# THE BAGHDAD DECLARATION

## By

## LIONEL ROSS

Also by the author: -
**Fine Feathers**
978-0-9552404-2-3

**Hidden Heritage**
978-0-9552404-1-6

# The Baghdad Declaration

ISBN 978-0-9552404-3-0

Published by:
i2i Publishing
Enterprise House
3b Middleton Road
Crumpsall
Manchester M8 5DT. UK
www.i2ipublishing.co.uk

**Somewhere in Iraq.**
Craig awoke with a start. As he opened his eyes he expected to see his familiar possessions in the billet in Basra. But instead there was blackness all around him and he realised he was hurting. No, he wasn't exactly in agony, but his legs and arms and almost his entire body were all very sore. Gingerly he stretched out his limbs; yes everything seemed to be working, but how it all ached.
*Where the hell was he?* He pondered in his stupefied state of half awake, half asleep. He stretched out his arms hoping to touch some identifiable object and realised he was lying on cool dry sand. Full consciousness was returning to him and now, relatively alert, he decided to try and stand up. The ache in his back made even forcing his body into a sitting position a painful manoeuvre. *Why the hell was it so dark?* He clambered to his feet and cautiously circled the area where he had been lying, but all he discovered was sand and impenetrable blackness. And then suddenly there was the feeling that memories were about to return. He knew with every fibre of his being that these memories would be unpleasant ones. Apart from being trapped in pitch-blackness and aching all over he was certain that something else was wrong and far, far worse than his own present predicament. But what was it?
Craig remembered that the jeep had been on its way to rendezvous with US troops coming south

from Faluja. Craig and his three mates had been off-duty in Basra, relaxing in the billet, when the four of them had been told to report to the main control centre. There they were told that they were to take part in an operation to flush out a small group of Sunni insurgents holed up in an old house further north. Craig and his group were early and had stopped the vehicle near to a large mound in the desert. Craig used this quiet road quite frequently as a short cut. This was contrary to his instructions to stay on the main highways, but he liked the lack of other military vehicles on this road and had never seen insurgents or heard of ambushes by them in this backwater. The mound intrigued Craig and its strange shape always fascinated him. There were many mounds in the desert but this one was different. It resembled a flat-topped pyramid. Craig always wondered what, if anything, in such a barren area could lie beneath it.

Now more specific memory was returning. He recalled jumping out of the jeep. His three companions from the 9 Regiment of the Royal Artillery were unpacking provisions for a quick bite of lunch before meeting up with the Americans.

Craig had always displayed far more curiosity than was good for him. His parents in Denton near Manchester had always told him that. So had his teachers. Now his officers were forever telling him the same thing. Healthy curiosity was one thing but his always seemed to get him into trouble.

Craig was a tall young man. His boyish good looks, intelligence and quiet charm had marked him out for early promotion. *If only I had stayed on at school,* he often mused, *I could have been an officer by now. Anyway, being a sergeant was nothing to be ashamed of,* he reassured himself. Craig loved the army.

He had always been a good team player and although many of the other lads were well into their twenties, he had captained the local football side when only seventeen years old. Craig was liked by all the boys and equally popular with the female fans when they came to cheer on their favourites. He would have been flattered and not a little embarrassed had he been able to hear some of the comments between the local girls as they admired his lithe, muscular body.

Suddenly he remembered that he had decided to take a walk to the mound.

'Hey Guys,' he had said to his three companions, 'while you get the grub ready I am going for a quick pee behind that mound.'

'Ok, Serge,' his friend Corporal Andy Jackson had said and off Craig had strolled.

He was of course aware, as they all were, of the ever-present danger of ambushes and roadside bombs. He had previously lost two very goods friends in that way. However, he pondered, apart from the mound the terrain is perfectly flat. We should spot approaching trouble in plenty of time to deal with it. Anyway, Andy Jackson was on watch while the two privates, Lee and Jameson, sorted out the food. Andy was a good reliable soldier and a close friend and Craig had no hesitation in leaving his radio with Andy in case Basra wished to transmit further instructions to the men.

The first thing Craig had to do was to cautiously encircle the mound to ensure that no one was hidden behind it. The sandy terrain looked as if it had been undisturbed for months, if not years. Craig was an experienced desert tracker and knew exactly what telltale signs to look for.

Then, in a blinding flash, he remembered the rest of the story. No wonder he felt that something really terrible had happened. Now he knew that something terrible had happened.

The call of nature had not been just an excuse to inspect the mound. It was genuine and the result of drinking far too much of the Arab coffee that was proving to be an even stronger addiction than his favourite lager back home in Manchester. However, as soon as he had relieved himself, he had decided to climb up the hidden side of the mound. He was almost at the top when he heard the explosion. It had come from the front of the mound where the jeep was parked. *Oh Jesus,* he thought, as he started to slide down, *my mates, what have those bastards done to my mates?*

And then suddenly he was falling. Half way down the slope a large section of the mound had given way. Craig had hit the ground flat on his back and that was the last he remembered until he awoke aching in the blackness.

Craig had no way of knowing how much time had passed since the explosion. He felt for his watch, but it must have been loosened and lost in the fall.

Then he remembered his gun and backpack. *They must be here somewhere,* he decided.

*But why was it so bloody dark?* He pondered. Once again he began to explore and this time with a growing sense of urgency. He had to get out of this place and find out what had happened to his friends. Craig reached into his breast pocket for his mobile cell phone. This was not army issue and was one of the latest versions featuring, in addition to telephonic communication, a camera with a high pixel rating and many other facilities. All these extra features worked well, but much of the time it was useless for its main purpose of contacting anyone by telephone. Not surprisingly, in the middle of the Iraqi desert, areas where a signal could be obtained were few and far between. Craig switched on the phone and found that, as he had expected, it was totally useless as a means of communication. If only he had the radio, he mused. He was becoming more and more desperate to learn the fate of his three companions.

The flames from the burning jeep had been quickly spotted by a helicopter on its way to give aerial support to the combined US & British troops, involved in the same operation. A fire tender, ambulance and three Saxon wheeled Armoured Personnel vehicles were dispatched to the scene. Sadly a scene of utter devastation greeted them. All that was left of the jeep was a charred and twisted chassis and of the occupants, just a few unidentifiable human remains. There had been four men in the vehicle when it set off and with pitifully little evidence to confirm or deny, the army was satisfied that all four members must have perished. It was quickly established that the jeep had been at the receiving end of a rocket, fired by insurgents from some distance away. Unfortunately the men did not have a chance to defend themselves. Death and destruction had hit them so swiftly that they must have died instantaneously. Four fine brave young soldiers in the prime of life or so the army thought. The army had no more idea than he had at that time, that Sergeant Craig Blackburn had escaped the fate of his compatriots and was lying unconscious deep inside the mound. By nightfall the wreck had been removed and what was considered to represent the charred remains of the four soldiers was placed in coffins for repatriation to the UK and burial.

The pitch-black desert night gave way to a bright dawn. Craig had discovered that the interior of the mound was much larger than he had appreciated from the exterior. He could still see virtually nothing in the darkness until, glancing back over his shoulder, he could discern a growing area of light some one hundred metres behind him. Turning round he started to run back towards the newly illuminated area. The welcome brightness he could now see was coming from what he took to be a window some four metres above him. Now he could identify the walls that had imprisoned him so successfully and protected him from the fate of his companions. He was in a huge cave with large rock walls and no, there was no window. The light he had seen was sunlight streaming in from a large jagged hole in the wall of the cave.

Suddenly Craig realised, this was where he must have fallen through. There had obviously been a weakness in the rock formation at that point and the explosion had loosened it.

*Oh my God,* he thought, *the explosion. Where are my mates?*

*I've got to get out of this place.*

Something caught his eye lying on the sandy ground near where he was standing. It was his watch and it told him that it was 6.30 am. Stepping back to retrieve it his foot struck another larger object. It was his backpack and just a few centimetres away he saw his gun partially immersed in the soft sand. Craig knelt down to recover his belongings and as he carefully retrieved the weapon, he felt other hard objects just below the surface. Hoping that there might be something here to help him to climb up the sheer jagged edges of the cave wall, he started to remove the sand from the immediate area. That was easy and quick work as the sand was soft and bone dry. In just a few minutes he had uncovered a heavy wooden table and incredibly enough four heavy beautifully carved chairs.

Craig was normally full of curiosity but his only purpose in continuing to dig was to find enough articles to aid his escape. Not for one minute did he forget the explosion the previous day and he dug frantically. In the end he discovered another smaller table and he realised that if he stood the smaller table on the larger one he could probably heave himself through the hole in the wall.

However, before he had dug out the smaller table he had found what looked like two scrolls of parchment. Craig put these aside with just a cursory glance. If he had found the crown jewels or the Holy Grail at that time they would have held no interest for him. He wanted to get out of this cave and find out if his mates were safe.

## 1191. Baghdad.

It was early morning when he arrived. Both the Muslims and the Jews had just finished their first prayers of the day and returned from the many Mosques and Synagogues of the city. The visitor was obviously important. He was accompanied by two servants and was quickly ushered into the courtyard.

'I have an important message from his Excellency the Caliph for his Excellency the Exilarch,' he instructed the servant. 'Pray ask him to grant me an immediate audience.'

'And your name, honoured sir?' the servant replied.

'I am the Vizier Abdul ibn Ali.'

The Exilarch was Daniel ben Hasdai. He was the acknowledged leader of the ancient Jewish community of Baghdad. He had inherited the title Exilarch or Resh Galuta from his father and he from his father, going back countless generations. He was determined to restore the ancient glory of the office whose incumbents could trace their bloodline all the way back to David, King of Israel.

An-Nasir was the Caliph of Baghdad. He was a Sunni Muslim and he too was determined to restore the ancient glory of his office.

There were a number of difficulties in the way of both of these men's ambitions.

To the east were the Seljuks. The Caliph had formed a pact with the Khwarizm Shah, Tekish, to attack the Seljuks. However, after the successful campaign against the Seljuks, Tekish had been so offended by the behaviour of one of the Caliph's viziers, that he had turned on his former ally and attacked and routed the Caliph's army.

Further still to the East was an even greater threat; Genghis Khan and his Mongol hordes. An-Nasir had tried to enlist the help of Genghis Khan in dealing with the offensive of the Seljuks and of Khwarezm under Tekish, but all he had succeeded in doing was bringing forward the day when Genghis Khan would attack Baghdad itself. Fortunately that was still some years in the future.

To the West lay the Holy Land. There, Saladin was locked in a never-ending series of battles with the Crusaders from Western Europe. Richard I of England, one of their leaders, after peace negotiations had once more failed, had brutally slaughtered three thousand Muslim prisoners. In the eyes of these Princes of Islam the Crusaders from the west were brutish barbarians, little different from their Mongol enemies to the East.

Saladin had asked for help from An-Nasir who, as a result of his own problems, was in no fit state to give any serious support.

The Caliphate of Baghdad and the Exilarchate of the Jews of Baghdad had worked closely together through most of the last three hundred years. On a personal level the Caliph considered the Exilarch to be a useful ally and a man who he could count upon as a friend. In the Baghdad of the Caliphate it was well known that the Exilarch was a direct descendant of the Israelite Kings, David and Solomon. These Kings were also recognised as significant prophets in Islam. The Jews posed no problem to the Caliphate. They were peaceful and hard working and had contacts with other Jewish communities throughout the known world. This in itself was very useful, as the Caliph knew he could rely on them in matters of trade reaching well beyond the areas of Muslim rule.

It was no surprise therefore in October 1191, soon after the Jewish New Year, that a messenger of the Caliph was sent to summon the Exilarch to a meeting in the Royal Palace the following week. Somehow or other the Baghdad rumour machine soon discovered that an important conference was to take place between the Jews and the Caliph, the Sunni ruler of Baghdad and of much of present day Iraq. The sympathies of the smaller community of Shi'a Muslims in the city lay with the Khwarezm, whom they hoped to assist in removing the Sunnis from the Caliphate. Once their leaders heard that an important meeting was to take place they set about denouncing both the Sunnis and the Jews in their Mosques.

The Caliph was in no position to deal with an insurgency in his own backyard and it was decided that they would change venue to one that could be kept secret. Far off in the desert, many miles to the south, on the road to Basra was the cave of Ibrahim. The Caliph had maintained a garrison there for many years. Historically, it was, according to local tradition, one of the resting places used by Abraham on his biblical journey from Chaldea towards Syria and the Holy Land.

The Caliph himself was unable to leave Baghdad without once again arousing the suspicions of the Shi'a Muslims. He summoned his brother, a man well known to the Exilarch.

'Yes, my dear brother,' Harun el Jabbar had said with a broad smile as soon as the Caliph's servants and advisors had been dismissed from their presence.

'Firstly, dear brother, how are you and your family? Does all go well for you?' the Caliph enquired. He had three other brothers and five sisters but rarely saw them and beyond being sure of their material welfare, he took little or no interest in them. Harun was different. Even as boys they had been close friends and the Caliph knew that if there was just one person in the world who would never let him down, Harun was that person.

'Through the blessings of Allah I am well and ready to help my beloved brother in whatever way he wishes.'

The Caliph assumed a serious expression as he explained the reasons for this meeting.

'My dear brother, Allah is testing us. Enemies surround us. I sent gifts to the accursed Tekish, the Khwarizm Shah and instead of gratefully accepting my tokens of friendship, he treacherously attacked our small army and routed them.'

'That much I know, my dear brother,' Harun replied.

Looking even more troubled the Caliph continued, 'I am trying to forge alliances and I have now despatched emissaries to the barbarian Genghis Khan. I do not trust these godless Mongols but we need their help.'

'Our friend Saladin is also in trouble in the Holy Land,' the Caliph explained. 'He has asked me for help to protect Al-Kuds (Jerusalem) from the Western barbarians, the accursed Crusaders. But what can we do for him when the enemies of Baghdad are threatening us at all sides.'

'We need to build up our army and that needs money,' the Caliph continued. 'Saladin may be our friend, but I fear he will lose the Holy land and we need to have allies there, not Crusaders.'

'I have also despatched emissaries to the Eastern Christians in Constantinople. They have no more love for the Western barbarians than we have, but they will not wage war on their Christian brothers on our behalf.'

'My brother,' Harun replied, 'what can I do to help you in these terrible times?'

'If Saladin loses the Holy Land,' the Caliph explained, 'I would rather have Jews there than Christians, even Eastern ones.'

Harun gasped. There had been no Jewish state in the Holy Land for a thousand years. The Jews had no army but they had one tremendous advantage. Their people were scattered throughout the known world and they were in a unique position to handle, as they did, many matters of trade and state.

'With the help of Allah, Saladin may prevail, but it looks increasingly less likely with every piece of news coming from the Holy Land.' the Caliph grimly told his brother.

'What I wish to do,' he continued, 'is to promise the Jews that their rights will be respected in the Holy land to the extent of setting up a small Jewish Kingdom under the Exilarch. This is dependent on their financial support for Baghdad. That way I could build an extensive fighting force to drive out the Western Infidels myself and retake all of the Holy Land in the name of Islam.'

'The Empire of the Caliphate would then stretch from the two rivers of Iraq to the Great Sea. And I will go down in history as the Caliph who drove out the accursed Crusaders.'

'That is a truly amazing plan,' Harun replied. 'So there would be, Allah being praised, a return to our past glory.'

'Yes,' the Caliph continued, 'That is the plan and I need you to talk to the Exilarch far away from those traitors to Islam, the Shi'a.'

'But exactly what am I to promise the Exilarch of the Jews?' Harun enquired.

'A kingdom in the Holy Land,' his brother replied.

'The Exilarch will want more detail than that, my brother,' Harun gently countered.

'If I am to achieve this agreement, I am sure you will want me to be more specific.'

'Try to be as vague as possible, but I know these people are not fools,' the Caliph replied.

'I will have our scribes draw up a parchment document stating that in return for the financial support for the Caliphate by world Jewry, we will look favourably on the establishment of a Jewish Kingdom in the Holy Land.' He continued. 'The fact that they will have a document making the undertaking in writing, should impress our friend Daniel ben Hasdai. You must remember that the Jews hate the Crusaders as much as we do. Look how they slaughtered countless thousands of them on their way to the East.'

'The idea of an alliance with the Caliphate will appeal to their sense of history.

Once we have conquered the territory we will certainly give them a piece of land for their Kingdom but only as a small part of our glorious Caliphate.'

So the meeting was arranged at the cave of Ibrahim, the ancestor of both the Jews and the Arabs. Undoubtedly this was a most appropriate venue.

## 2006.

### The Cave of Ibrahim.

Craig had great difficulty in dragging the large table to a point under the hole in the rock face. It took two hours and almost superhuman strength to achieve this. Not only was the table incredibly heavy, but also the soft dry sand was seriously impeding his efforts. Eventually he succeeded and was then left with the not much easier task of dragging and pulling the smaller table. This had to be lifted on to the top of the larger table and when Craig achieved this, the combined weight was forcing the legs of the larger table deeper into the dry powdery sand. He could only climb on to the top once he was sure the whole structure was level and would not tumble over to hurl him again into the sand. Craig recovered his backpack and gun and started to climb up. Then the smaller table wobbled and Craig's efforts were rewarded with just what he had feared, another fall. Fortunately, the softness of the sandy ground ensured that he did not suffer further damage.

He had however, landed near the two scrolls of parchment and while regaining his wind after the previous exertion he decided to investigate what they could be. The first one he opened was written in beautiful ornate flowing classical Arabic script such as Craig had seen in the Koran and other documents. The other scroll had also been produced with loving care. The script, however, was quite different and resembled the Hebrew block characters he had often seen in newscasts from Israel.

Craig was intrigued to discover the subject matter of the scrolls, but his main purpose was to escape from his rocky prison and find out the fate of his comrades. He decided to quickly photograph the texts of the two scrolls with his camera/phone. This was an easy job as the bright desert light was now streaming down from the hole in the cave wall and illuminating a patch of the floor just near to where he had fallen.

Then he placed the two scrolls on one of the wooden chairs and began to climb again. This time he managed to grab the jagged rocky edge of the opening and although in agony from the sharp rock cutting in to his hands, he managed to lever himself up to the opening. As he swung himself into a sitting position he could see the desert outside and how peaceful and undisturbed it looked; just like yesterday. Craig easily slid down the sand covered slope to the ground and trotted round to the road facing section of the mound. The road was some hundred metres away and as he approached he could see that his own worst fears were to be confirmed. Of the jeep there was no sign, but the earth around where he had last seen it was burned to a deadly black. A few stunted shrubs that had been alongside the road were also charred almost beyond recognition. The area of devastation was large enough to indicate a serious fire and Craig knew that his compatriots could never have survived.

Craig was now desperate to get back to base. He sat down by the roadside to consider his position. He was at least twenty miles from Basra. Although he felt sick with the knowledge of what had happened, he was hungry and becoming progressively thirstier as the burning Iraqi sun beat down on him. He eagerly consumed at least half of his water supply and some emergency rations from his backpack. Craig knew that if the heat of the sun did not cause him to die from dehydration there was a distinct danger that insurgents would spot him walking along the road and he would become one of the frequently publicised kidnap victims of these fanatics. *To catch a British soldier would really be a great prize for them,* he mused.

Craig knew the road well and realised there was only one sensible course of action. He must return to the mound and wait for nightfall in the cool of the cave. Then he could set out for the long walk back to Basra. Every now and again he vainly tried the phone but there was no signal.

The far side of the mound was facing north and protected from the sun, although Craig knew that this would no longer be the case later in the afternoon. He wondered whether there was an easier way to re-enter the cave. Whoever had brought the tables and chairs and the scrolls must have had a better means of access. Then Craig realised that the distance from the ground on the inside of the opening was much greater than on the outside. Sand must have been blowing against this North facing wall for maybe hundreds of years and piling up. Perhaps there was another entrance and it was buried.

Craig decided to give himself an hour to find another point of entry and if this was unsuccessful he would just have to climb up and jump in where he had previously fallen in to the cave. He had no spade to dig away the sand, but here was a whole new use for his rifle butt. After toiling in the intense desert heat for fifty-five minutes, he had virtually given up on the idea, when he uncovered an area of impacted sand in the newly revealed base of the rock. He started feverishly to hack away at this area and toiled for another hour in the searing heat before being rewarded by more of the soft dry sand similar to that within the cave. Then suddenly the ground of the area he had uncovered gave way and he could see enough of a tunnel to allow him to crawl through. And yes, just a minute later he was back in the now so welcome cooler air of the cave.

Craig had been so desperate to escape from the cave earlier and now he was glad to be back within its confines. Not only would it protect him from the heat, but in addition he would be out of the sight of any insurgents travelling in the vicinity. Although in the past he had never encountered any trouble in this area, there was no doubt that there now were insurgents in the region. Had they not murdered his friends just one day earlier? At last, night fell and this time the darkness was more than welcome to Craig. The scrolls were not large, about twenty centimetres long and at first he considered taking them with him. Some sort of instinct, however, told him that this was not a good idea. And so, Craig left his cave and commenced the long walk back to Basra.

## 1196.

### The Cave of Ibrahim.

The cave was hidden under a rocky protuberance in the desert and was home to a small force of Baghdadi soldiers under their captain Feisal ibn Mansur.

They were hardly an effective fighting force. At best they were more of an early warning of incursions from the East and South. Four-hour watches were detailed and two men were ordered to climb up to the top of the mound and maintain surveillance of the surroundings in the burning sun or the freezing cold desert night.

When a messenger arrived to alert Captain Feisal to the expected visit in just two days time of his Excellency Harun el Jabbar, the brother of the Caliph together with the Exilarch of the Jews, Daniel ben Hasdai, he was sworn to secrecy as to the identity of the important visitors. Most of his soldiers had been with him for years and he would have trusted them with his life. The newest recruit to this small band was Hussein ibn Ali. He was an obedient soldier who carried out his duties efficiently and had been a member of this group for just two months. He was known to be a Shi'a Muslim, but he had sworn allegiance to the Caliph and his loyalty was not suspected to the slightest degree by the captain. There were many Shi'a Muslims in the service of the Caliph and they were fine soldiers and usually loyal to Baghdad. It was not known how many of them, in their heart of hearts longed to see a Shi'a on the throne, but many of them had still died bravely facing the forces of their co-religionists the Seljuks and the Khwarizm Sultan, Tekish. In any case neither the Khwarezm nor the Seljuks were Arabs. Muslims yes, Shi'a yes, but not Arabs like the Baghdadi population.

The first of the eminent visitors to arrive was the Exilarch with his small entourage. This consisted of a Rabbi, a scribe and two Jewish soldiers assigned to them by the Palace of the Caliph for this journey. There were also many Jews in the army of the Caliph. They made fine soldiers and were often found among the officer ranks where they displayed imagination, determination and considerable organisational skills. All of the party of the Exilarch wore travelling clothes. The garments in no way identified them either as Jews or as men of any particular importance. The robes they wore were the typical clothing of merchants who travelled, usually by camel, to sell their wares in the far-flung towns of the Middle East. Captain Feisal knew immediately who the visitors were. He had been told to expect them and despite their unimpressive appearance he greeted them with all the dignity that should be shown to honoured guests of the Caliph.

A corner of the huge cave had been prepared for the Jewish contingent. The Exilarch Daniel ben Hasdai, the Rabbi, Elazar ben Moshe and the scribe, Yosef HaSofer settled themselves down to wait for the Caliph's emissary to arrive. They did not have to wait long. Soon they could hear the sound of the voice of Captain Feisal instructing his men to line-up outside the cave to greet the Caliph's brother and his companions.

They too wore the clothing of travelling merchants, but Harun el Jabbar was well known. He was, after all, the Caliph's brother and as such received a warm but respectful welcome from the small garrison.

A large table had been prepared for the meeting in the centre of the cave and the two groups lost no time in starting their negotiations. First however, the best food obtainable was offered to the distinguished guests. Two of the soldiers had been despatched to Basra the previous day to obtain kosher food for the Jews. This was equally acceptable to the Muslims with their similar dietary laws. The Caliph had instructed that everything that could be done should be done to make his Jewish guests comfortable and at ease.

Harun started the meeting by welcoming the Exilarch and his party.

Daniel had been more than a little intrigued as he had tried to consider what the reason for the meeting might be.

*First,* he had pondered, *the Caliph asks me to attend on him in Baghdad. Then he cancels the audience and asks me to meet with his brother miles away to the South.*

The Exilarch, Daniel, decided to speak up as soon as the unusually fulsome welcome was complete.

'It is a great honour to be in the company of the illustrious brother of his Excellency the Caliph,' he ventured, smiling broadly to acknowledge that this was a friendly remark and should be taken as such. .

'May I respectfully enquire the reason for the meeting and why it was necessary for it to take place miles from Baghdad and under such conditions of secrecy?'

'Of course, Your Excellency the Exilarch,' Harun answered, also smiling broadly.

'His Excellency the Caliph An-Nasir, my beloved ruler and brother, feels that the exile of the Jews from their homeland has been of far too long a duration.'

The Exilarch and his two companions were astonished to hear these words coming from the lips of the Caliph's brother and emissary. The Jewish community of Babylon and of the area of Iraq had been in existence for well over a thousand years. Most of the time they had lived in peace and reasonable comfort with their Muslim neighbours. However, they were never allowed to forget, nor would they wish to, that they were exiles from the land of Israel and Judea many miles away to the West. Moreover, they were in Islamic terms, a subject people and could never expect the full rights accorded to their Muslim neighbours.

The Exilarch recovered his composure and replied,

'It is true our exile has been long and hard. We are honoured and happy to be in Baghdad but we have always yearned to return to our own land of Zion and Jerusalem.'

Harun continued, 'the infidels of the West are in the Holy Land. Our brother Saladin who fought this rabble with so much success is now in deep trouble. The Crusaders are threatening to take the holy city that you call Jerusalem and we call Al Kuds (the sacred.). If these barbarians succeed they will slaughter every Muslim and every Jew they find. Do you know that King Richard of England, one of the leaders of the Crusade, had three thousand Muslim prisoners murdered near Jaffa just two months ago?'

Daniel nodded sympathetically. He knew plenty about the activities of the Crusaders.

'These same people,' he added, 'on their way through Europe have slaughtered tens of thousands of our people in town after town as they passed by on their way to the Holy Land.'

'So,' Harun continued, 'we both know we have a common enemy. My brother, the Caliph, wishes to send a large army to the Holy Land to drive these invaders into the sea. However,' Harun explained, 'we have plenty of trouble awaiting us in the East. Apart from the Khwarizm Shah and the Seljuks there is the increasing problem of the Mongols under Genghis Khan.'

'Anyway, my friend,' Harun continued, 'the most holy task and the most pressing is for us to turn our attention to the Holy Land. Don't you agree?'

'Of course I agree,' Daniel replied, deeply moved, 'but what can we Jews do? We would be very happy to help, but we have no army of our own and we are a people scattered to the four corners of the world.'

'Tell me, my friend Daniel, if I might address you by your first name,' Harun answered with a thoughtful expression on his face. 'If we really worked together, the Jews and the Muslims, a great army could be raised to liberate your brothers and mine in the Holy land. My beloved brother, the Caliph, has given me a document guaranteeing the people of Israel the right to a Kingdom in your old ancestral home. What we need from you is to raise a large sum of money from your people all over the world to help finance the great army of which we speak.'

'What a wonderful dream,' the Exilarch answered. 'The idea is bold and beautiful. However, the Exilarch is no longer the acknowledged ruler of world Jewry as in days gone by. There are strong and independent communities in such places as Spain and France and Germany who are unlikely to take my request very seriously. A few hundred years ago when the whole Jewish world revolved around Babylon, the situation would have been very different. I would like to help, more than anything else in this world, but I need to consider how our aim could be achieved.'

Harun had not expected such a negative reaction to the proposition and he looked, as indeed he felt, deeply disappointed.

The two men and their advisors sat in silence wrapped in their own thoughts until Daniel spoke again,

'May I please hear the terms of the document that your esteemed brother, the Caliph, has prepared?'

'Of course,' Harun answered, sensing a possible breakthrough. He opened both of the two scrolls lying on the table.

The one written in classical Hebrew he passed across to the Exilarch and he then proceeded to read from the one written in classical Arabic:

*'In the eleventh year of the reign of An-Nasir, Abbasid Caliph of Baghdad, may the blessings of Allah and his prophet Mohamed be upon him.*

*It is agreed that in exchange for the financial support of the people of Israel and Judea scattered throughout the known world, in the liberation of the Holy Land from the Infidel Crusaders, that his Excellency the Caliph of Baghdad will look favourably upon the re-establishment of a Jewish Kingdom in the Holy Land and the re-settlement of all Jews who wish to do so, within the Kingdom.*

The Arabic scroll followed on with an additional declaration. Harun saw no point in reading this out to the Jews, as it did not directly concern them. The second declaration read as follows: -

*It is also agreed that apart from the proposed Kingdom of the Jews, the entire region stretching from the two*

*rivers to the Great Sea will be under the rule of a Sunni Caliphate as the only true representative of the Holy Prophet Mohammed and his Holy Koran. All blasphemous attempts to adhere to the heresy of Shi'a Islam are to be utterly destroyed.*

This was probably the most emotional moment in the life of Daniel ben Hasdai. He had never even begun to dream that he would one day hear such a declaration and his eyes filled with tears as he imagined the splendour of a new Kingdom of Judea. He wanted to say a prayer there and then to thank the Almighty for choosing him, one of the lesser Exilarchs, to receive this declaration.

He read the Hebrew scroll through carefully and somehow the words, *'look favourably'* stood out and quickly caused him to rein in his enthusiasm. This was hardly a guarantee that the Caliph would actually establish a Jewish Kingdom in the Holy Land. In addition where in the Holy Land would this kingdom be established, if, indeed it was? Would it include Jerusalem? How many Jews would the Caliph actually allow to return and how many would wish to do so?

Daniel ben Hasdai was, however, a diplomat.

Turning to his two companions, the Rabbi and the Scribe, he said,

'This is indeed a special moment in the history of our people. This offer must be considered very seriously, but I would never like to promise support to a great man like his Excellency the Caliph An-Nasir unless I knew I could provide what he needs for this Holy project.'

Addressing Harun el Jabbar once again he continued,

'Excellency, we cannot thank your esteemed brother enough for this offer. We will also pray that every blessing the Lord can bestow will be granted to him and his family. We will now return to Baghdad and start to despatch messengers to all major parts of the Jewish world in a serious endeavour to take up this wonderful offer. My friend Harun, if I may call you that, please assure the Caliph of our gratitude and loyalty and within four months I hope to be able to accept the proposal.'

Harun was feeling deeply disappointed. He wanted to show his brother an immediate successful outcome to the meeting, but he now knew this was not possible.

Arising with his entourage he intoned,

'May the blessings of Allah be upon you and we must all pray for a satisfactory conclusion to this whole matter.'

The three Jews prepared to leave with their two-man escort and as soon as they had departed from the cave Harun instructed Captain Feisal to carefully bury the two scrolls in the soft sand adjacent to one of the walls of the cave.

Harun had known the Captain for many years and knew him to be a loyal and efficient soldier. He needed someone he could trust to voice his concerns to over the outcome of the meeting and invited the Captain to join him.

The two men had been talking for at least half an hour when they heard noises from outside the cave. The other nine men from the garrison and Harun's two travelling companions were nowhere to be seen as they came out of the cave into the bright sunlight to investigate. As they adjusted to the piercingly bright sunlight of the desert afternoon they took in a sight that was almost too horrifying to behold. A group of some forty Shi'a Muslims from the East were wiping the blood from their swords and looking down with savage satisfaction at the bodies of the garrison soldiers and Harun's two personal guards. Then Harun noticed that standing in the midst of this gang of killers was Hussein ibn Ali, the newest and only Shi'a recruit to the now destroyed garrison.

Hussein stepped forward, sword in hand, and addressed Harun.

'Thus shall die all traitors to Islam. A pact with the accursed Jews, what more could we expect from those who defame the name of our holy prophet and his family. Your brother will soon be replaced by a Shi'a Caliph and my men and I will now execute you and your Captain in the name of Allah.'

And so perished Harun el Jabbar, brother and emissary of the Caliph of Baghdad, and the cave of Ibrahim returned to the desert from whence it came.

## 2006.
### Basra Bound.

Craig took a few sips of his now sadly depleted water supply and nibbled away at most of the remainder of his desert emergency rations. Feeling rested after his enforced stay inside the cave, he marched briskly along in the cool night air. He had never become used to the huge swings in temperature that the desert provided. By day anything from forty to fifty degrees Celsius was normal but at night the thermometer plunged to as little as five or six degrees. Still the cold air was a blessing as he negotiated the long walk back to Basra. He had wondered if the British forces would be searching for him but he had long since realised that they would almost certainly have assumed he had perished with his comrades.

Craig calculated that he must have covered about half of the distance and decided to stop at the side of the road for a rest. He had walked in the still dark of the night alongside the road but not actually on it so that he could hide if he heard a vehicle that may belong to insurgents. His ears were constantly straining for the sound of movement. Had he been on the main road some miles to the west he would certainly have been picked up by a patrol by now. However, this whole nightmare had only come to pass because he had taken the short cut on this quiet pock marked and rubble-strewn road that passed the strange mound. Otherwise, his companions would still have been alive and he would probably have been safe inside the billet in Basra. Craig knew he would be in deep trouble with the army when he eventually returned. But this was nothing in comparison to the deep guilt he felt for being responsible for his comrades' deaths.

He never heard a thing. Maybe he had dozed off momentarily but there was no doubt that someone was holding a knife to his throat and muttering in heavily accented Arabic English for him to put his hands behind his back. His backpack was on the ground beside him and the rifle had already been lifted from the ground before he knew what was happening. There were four of them. His hands were tied behind his back and he was blindfolded as he was pushed and propelled towards an ancient Land Rover some five hundred metres away. How they had seen him sitting in a hollow at the side of the road was beyond his comprehension. Equally beyond his comprehension was how he had not heard them approaching. But they had him and in common with so many other European hostages that would probably be the last the world would know of Sergeant Craig Blackburn.

What a coup, he bitterly decided. To actually capture a British soldier. Civilians of all kinds were fair game to these people but a British soldier; that was a real bonus.

Eventually the car stopped and he was roughly escorted into a building. His blindfold and outer clothing were removed and he was flung into a small, dirty, stuffy room with no windows. The only light came from a single light bulb hanging from a dusty piece of ancient flex.

He quickly discovered his captor's names were Ali, Mahmoud, Fuad and Usama.

'Ma ismok?' (What is your name?) Mahmoud demanded. Ali who spoke a little English then repeated the question in Craig's mother tongue. This information Craig supplied. It was hardly a secret as it was clearly stated together with his rank on his uniform and in his backpack. The other three kidnappers being unable to communicate simply yelled at him in Arabic. Ali told him with a combination of the few English words that he possessed and sign language that they were from a Sunni group determined to install a Sunni Islamic government in Iraq. The country would then be controlled by Shari'a (Islamic Law) as interpreted by the strict criteria of the Wahabi sect of Saudi Arabia.

The four of them repeatedly cursed the Shi'a Muslims, the Christians, the US and the UK who they called Crusaders, the Jews and the Israelis who they called Zionists and Saddam Hussein, as if he was still in power. The only Arabic Craig knew, apart from greetings, was curses and these were definitely very unpleasant ones.

Two of his four captors stayed in the room with him at all times. They had long discussions in Arabic that he was, of course, unable to understand. Sometimes their conversations became heated and the one called Fuad would become very agitated. Craig's ankles were manacled and his wrists handcuffed. They fed him and gave him drinks. But then, kidnappers did not usually starve their victims. They took him into the adjoining toilet, a filthy evil smelling closet. They watched him perform his required bodily functions and then quite gently pushed him back into the other room. .

Craig tried at first to get into conversation with the one called Ali but he showed no further desire to communicate and his English, and for that matter Craig's Arabic, were not up to the task.

Three days passed in this manner. Craig had plenty of time to think and brood. His family in Manchester would have been notified of his presumed death after the Jeep had exploded. He loved his family and was heart-broken that he should unwittingly be the cause of so much heartbreak and pain to them. He also had a girlfriend, Kirsty, and had resolved that on his next leave he would propose marriage. She would have been devastated to learn of his reported death.

His gun and backpack had been removed by the kidnappers and taken into another room. They also had taken his phone although as a means of communication it was useless. Well, Craig decided, they had a top prize, a British soldier and they could just bide their time before making known their demands.

It did occur to Craig on the third day that his captors were probably somewhat puzzled as to why there had been no announcement from the British authorities that a soldier was missing. They could hardly have known that in the eyes of the army he was already a dead man.

On the morning of the fourth day, Craig heard sounds of a serious argument coming from the other room. Mahmoud & Usama were with him and looked increasingly concerned by the hysterical shouting of their two comrades. Craig could now identify the individual voices of his four captors. The two kidnappers who were off duty from guarding him were Ali and Fuad. Ali usually spoke quietly and earnestly but he was shouting. As for Fuad, he sounded as if he was totally out of control. Mahmoud and Usama whispered together and glanced almost fearfully at the door from which the altercation appeared to originate. After a few minutes Usama rose and with a worried glance at Craig disappeared. Craig was in no position to attack the one remaining captor in the room and make his escape as he was still shackled, handcuffed and chained to the wall. After a further interminable seeming two or three minutes Ali came back into the room. His black hair was dishevelled and he was visibly shaking with what Craig initially took to be anger. He had the mobile cell phone in his hand and almost hurled himself upon Craig.

'What this garbage?' he screamed.

At first Craig could not understand what the Iraqi was talking about. Why would he call the latest instrument, garbage? Every Iraqi he had met and that was a very considerable number, either had or aspired to having a state of the art mobile cell phone that they could show off to their friends.

Craig tried to answer but realised that anything but the simplest explanation would not be understood.

'What this garbage?' Ali again yelled.

Craig decided to try. He could now see that in Ali's other hand had appeared a fierce looking knife. If he did not calm Ali down he was sure that Ali would kill him.

'Don't you like the phone?' he ventured. Craig was genuinely puzzled.

'No, this garbage,' Ali replied pointing to the screen of the phone.

All of a sudden Craig realised. They had been able to read some if not all of the Arabic in the photograph of the text from one of the scrolls. Whether it was this text or the Hebrew text in the other photograph that had caused the big upset, he had yet to decide.

'You Israeli spy?' Ali accused. So they had seen the Hebrew, Craig decided.

He was beginning to become irritated and very concerned by all this fuss. Still if they thought he was Israeli that would be even worse than being British in this predicament.

'I am a British soldier and my name is Craig Blackburn. You know all this already. That Hebrew is just from a photo of an old scroll I once found and so is the Arabic one.'

Mahmoud who had so far been a spectator to all of this ruse and crossed over to Ali.

He spoke quietly to him in Arabic as if he was trying to calm him down.

'Eyh da?' (What is that?) He enquired, turning to Craig and pointing to the two photos as he scrolled backwards and forwards between them on the phone's large screen.

Before Craig could say a word Ali launched into a long, emotional and convoluted speech. Craig, of course, understood not one word.

Suddenly, Ali collapsed onto the floor just as if all the air had been taken out of him.

He handed Mahmoud the phone and Mahmoud sat down besides him to read what the photograph of the Arabic script said. This was a difficult process as the ornate Arabic script was difficult to decipher and especially on such a small screen. As he read Mahmoud did not become angry, he just went paler and paler and eventually returned the phone to Ali as he burst into tears.

Craig knew that the two languages had many words in common but were written with entirely different script. He was sure that very few Iraqis would be able to read Hebrew. Craig had quickly recognised the script when he had first discovered the scrolls in the cave and he was fairly sure that most Arabs would also instantly recognise it as the language of the people they considered to be their sworn enemies. The people they recognised as the occupiers of the land belonging to their Palestinian brothers. Craig heard Ali say something that sounded like 'yahud' and then spat onto the floor. Craig knew that this was the Arabic word for Jew. Finally Usama and Fuad re-entered the room. Fuad was bleeding from a gash over his right eye and Craig quickly noticed that he seemed unable to move his right arm. It was obvious that Ali and Fuad had fought among themselves as they argued over the photographed documents before Ali had returned to the room where Craig was being held. .

Now they were ignoring Craig. He may just as well have not been there as they entered into a long and sometimes heated discussion. After what seemed like an eternity Usama and Fuad rose and left the room. Ali and Mahmoud talked some more and then once again, Ali tried to interrogate Craig about the photographs. He soon realised that this was impossible and seemed to be recovering his usual equilibrium. Mahmoud left the room and returned after a few minutes with coffee, pita and fruit for three. Craig had neither the ability nor the desire to converse and the other two seemed to be exhausted by the morning's activities. So they ate in silence.

By mid afternoon Craig was fairly certain that Usama and Fuad had left the small building. He began to wonder how he could escape the clutches of these fanatics while their numbers were depleted.

By nightfall there was no sign of the return of the two absent captors. Now there was rarely more than one kidnapper with him at any one time. If only they would leave him alone completely he could try to escape from the handcuffs and manacles. *Chance would be fine thing,* he decided. Eventually he drifted off to a sleep punctuated by frequent periods of painful wakefulness while he coped with cramp and the aches caused by spending too many days and nights on the hard floor.

Early the following morning he was awakened by the sound of voices coming from the other room. He was alone at last and took the opportunity to try and escape from his chains. The best chance appeared to be the handcuffs as they were large but alas not large enough for his hands to slide through. Then he noticed that his captors had left a soiled plate from the previous night's pita and that a pat of butter or margarine was on the plate. Quickly Craig manoeuvred himself into a position where he could rub his right hand on the greasy substance. Then he tried again to collapse his fingers into the smallest possible space in an endeavour to slide the handcuff over the hand. He tucked his thumb under his palm and pushed the cuff over the widest part of his hand and there it stuck. It would move neither up nor down and then the door opened and a strange man entered his prison.

'Salaam Aleikum,' the stranger greeted him.

Craig decided to respond informally to this greeting.

'Marhaba,' (Hello) he responded.

The man was of medium height and slim build. He was dressed in a navy suit with a matching spotted tie. His hair was dark and greying at the temples. He was clean-shaven unlike his captors who all sported long beards. His complexion was fairly dark but like many Arabs he could easily have passed for a Spaniard or an Italian.

The man spoke again and this time in English. His accent indicated that his mother tongue was Arabic but his pronunciation and vocabulary was as good as any Englishman and in fact was probably better than many of Craig's fellow countrymen.

'Marhaba. My name is Professor Abdullah Sa'id of the Baghdad Museum of the Caliphate.'

'May I know your name?' He enquired, just as if they were chatting at a social gathering.

*What on earth was this man doing here,* he wondered. *He certainly does not look like a kidnapper or a terrorist.*

'Yes Sir,' Craig answered, 'I am Sergeant Craig Blackburn of the 9 Regiment, Royal Artillery. Have you come to rescue me?'

'Come, come, good sir,' the Professor answered, 'you are not in prison. These men have just been looking after you. It is dangerous out there for a lone British soldier so they had restrained you only until you could be returned to the proper authorities.'

'Ali,' the Professor called through the slightly open door, 'Come and release our friend now. I will look after him and see he is brought back to where he should be.'

Ali entered and proceeded to unlock the handcuffs, noting with a smirk that the right hand was greasy and trapped.

He then removed the manacles and Craig slowly stood up and stretched his limbs.

'Why not have a wash before we leave?' the Professor suggested.

Despite all the fine words Ali still followed him into the toilet and then into the washroom and watched carefully as he tried to make some effort to clean himself up.

The Professor's car, a Mercedes of some age, but very impressive by Iraqi standards, was parked a short distance away. Craig quickly realised that his captivity had not ceased; it had just changed its nature. As he walked to the car side by side with the Professor he was well aware of the fact that close behind were Ali and Mahmoud. The Professor gestured to Craig to take the front seat while the two kidnappers jumped into the back.

Craig had some idea of their approximate location and was hoping that once on a main highway they would travel South towards Basra, but he was not altogether surprised to find that they were travelling North. The road was a poor road similar to that from where he had been captured and after an estimated twenty miles the Professor pulled off onto a rough track.

Craig was now sure he was still a prisoner but the large house that greeted them at the end of the track was completely unexpected.

'This does not look like my billet in Basra,' he ventured.

'Of course not, Craig my dear fellow,' the Professor answered affably.

'This is where I live and do most of my work.'

'Come inside. There is something I wish to discuss with you.'

With the two kidnappers behind him and not the faintest idea where he was, Craig had no choice. He seemed to have exchanged a filthy disgusting jail for another prison, albeit a rather more comfortable one.

## 1191.
### Overturned Plans.

The Exilarch, Daniel ben Hasdai and his companions were well on the way back to Baghdad when the murderous gang of Shi'a thugs had arrived at the cave of Ibrahim. However, news of the violent death of the Caliph's brother arrived in the city the following day. This was due to the return of a further two soldiers of the Caliph's army to the cave to relieve two other members of the garrison scheduled for home leave. They were greeted with a scene of wholesale slaughter and preceded with all speed to bury the rotting corpses of their fallen comrades. Then they recognised the body of Harun el Jabbar, the favourite brother of the Caliph. They decided to take his body back to

Baghdad, as they were sure that the Caliph would want his brother to have a state funeral.

As they worked at the gruesome task the two men wondered who had committed this foul crime. They knew there had been some kind of meeting held in the cave but they did not know the identity of the parties to this meeting. Had they known that the Exilarch, a Rabbi, a Scribe and two of the Caliph's loyal soldiers had been the visitors they would have been hard pressed to suspect that they could have slaughtered all of the garrison soldiers, Harun el Jabbar and his companions. As it transpired they were saved this conjecture through the bravery of Captain Feisal who, even in death, was a dedicated officer of the Caliph. There was a rock lying besides the body of the Captain and somehow he had managed to write in his own blood the words HUSSEIN IBN ALI- SHI'A to tell of the treachery that had befallen them.

The Caliph An-Nasir was a hard man but he was broken hearted to learn of the murder and hastened to bury the remains of his beloved brother in accordance with Islamic traditions. He quickly discovered that the Exilarch and his companions had been fortunate to escape just half an hour before the murderous band of assassins arrived. The Caliph decided that this whole affair was a sign from Allah that he should concentrate his attention on the threats from the East and that he should leave the problems of the Holy Land in the hands of Saladin.

As for the Jews, the story of the Baghdad Declaration lay buried in the sands of time in the cave of Ibrahim and was never mentioned again by the Exilarch and his advisors. That was until a certain British soldier in 2006………..

## 2006
### A Different Kind of Prison.

The house reminded Craig of a lesser British stately home, but the garden, if it could be called as such, was another matter. It was simply desert with a few stunted shrubs dotted around.

The four men entered the hallway and Craig was astonished to see figures and artefacts that would have been proud exhibits in the British Museum. *If this is the home of the Professor he must indeed be a wealthy man,* Craig thought.

'Now Craig,' the Professor said reassuringly, as they climbed the wide staircase to the upper floor. 'Please don't look so worried. Nobody here is going to harm you. Do you know that the British army thinks you are dead?'

This statement came as something of a shock to Craig. He had realised that the Army would have assumed he had perished with his companions, but he had not thought that his captors would already be aware of his identity or lack of it.

'Look Craig,' the Professor continued. 'My first name is Abdullah. I can tell you are an intelligent man. Although you are only a Sergeant,' he added, a little patronisingly, 'I want us to be friends. I think I will value your help far more than the somewhat unimaginative British army.'

'So,' Craig replied bitterly, 'I am still a prisoner.'

'Come now, my friend,' Abdullah answered, 'please do not look at it this way. I need your help and once the project I am working on is completed, you will be free to go.'

*I don't have a choice*, Craig decided.

They had now entered a large room on the first floor of the house. There were three impressive looking computers in the room, two of them being operated by young Iraqi men. However, it was the third occupant of the room who immediately caught and held Craig's attention. Craig was a prisoner, maybe in fairly luxurious surroundings, but a prisoner nonetheless. His plight receded, however, into the inner recesses of his mind as he looked at the captivatingly beautiful young woman standing before him.

She was probably thirty years old and of medium height. Her black hair was the perfect frame for her almond shaped face with its high cheekbones and sensuous dark brown eyes. The trouser suit she was wearing was modest enough to satisfy the propriety of any religious Muslim, but it could not hide the shapely contours of her delightful figure.

He promptly realised he was staring and managed a throaty 'Hello!'

'This is Leila,' Abdullah explained. 'She is Iraqi but has spent many years in America studying the history of the period that is my speciality; the Caliphate of Baghdad.'

This time Craig managed a stronger 'Hello' and a broad smile. 'I am Craig Blackburn of the British army stationed in Basra.'

'Ah,' she replied smiling mischievously, 'one of our occupiers.'

'Craig, please sit down with us,' Abdullah said with a frown in the direction of Leila.

There was a large table with eight chairs in the room and after sitting down at the head, Abdullah gestured to Leila and Craig to join him.

'Craig,' the Professor began, 'I want to know where the photos of the texts in your phone came from.'

Craig was determined not to be helpful.

'I don't remember exactly where,' he began. 'There were some old parchments lying under some sand that I found on one of my stops on my way back to Basra.'

'You must know where,' the Professor replied a little testily.

*One minute I am intelligent and the next minute he is talking to me like a naughty schoolboy,* Craig thought. *Well that is all he is going to get out of me.*

Then Leila spoke, 'Come on Craig, you can do better than that.'

Craig smiled again and responded, 'I really don't remember. I was lost and only had my compass to navigate with.'

'Anyway,' Craig decided to chance a little reciprocal questioning. 'What on earth is so special about them? They certainly caused a big upset with Ali and Fuad and the others.'

'Oh, they are just old government decrees,' Abdullah answered airily.

'So why so much interest?' Craig countered.

'We need to try to establish how old they are and the area in which you found them may give us a clue,' Leila explained.

'Well that is all I can tell you,' Craig answered leaning back in his seat.

The Professor then rose and approached one of the computers. Craig watched him and was surprised to see that the photographs had already been downloaded from his mobile cell phone onto the machine. Craig, although far from happy in his new captivity, could not help but admire the clarity of the pictures.

Obviously a man of the Professor's education would have no trouble in reading the beautiful ornamental Arabic script. The Professor turned towards Craig again and with a faint smile continued,

'I want you to try and remember where you found these documents. It is very important to my research.'

'I really can't remember,' Craig replied with as much certainty as he could muster.

With that, Abdullah rose and gestured impatiently for Craig to follow him. The Professor escorted him to a large luxurious bedroom and after promising to send him food and drink he departed. The room was elegantly furnished and would not have shamed a European five star hotel. Every creature comfort was provided including a modern en-suite bathroom. There was just one difference. The windows had bars and he had heard Abdullah lock the door when he left. He was still a captive.

**2006.**
**Somewhere in the Negev Desert.**
The message came through on a secure line and was automatically decoded by Jack's computer. At first he thought it was a joke. And then he realised

that the information came from one of their most reliable and levelheaded operatives in the field. He knew it must be given serious credence. Jack read and reread the message several times.

*Wow,* he thought, *this is dynamite. It must go straight to the top.*

Jack Baker was born in Prestwich, Manchester in 1974. He had attended a Zionist youth organisation at his local synagogue in his teens and that had cinched his resolve to settle in Israel as soon as he finished university. He had ultimately arrived there with a first class honours degree in Engineering Management. The Israeli army, where he was committed to carrying out his National Service, soon realised that Jack was ideal material for the intelligence service. He was invited to apply for a position with the Mossad and was then subject to an exhaustive series of gruelling interviews. Every facet of his past life and background was examined and re-examined. He passed all the tests and profiling with flying colours.

Currently Jack was posted to an information gathering post 'somewhere in the Negev desert.' This was the way the secret security post was usually described. His task was to receive reports from field agents and his particular area of responsibility covered such strategic territories as Southern Iraq, Kuwait and the Kurdish areas to the North of Iraq and Iran. His colleague, Yossi, looked after the Baghdad area, a full time occupation on its own.

So astonished was Jack by the contents of the report that, quite contrary to standing orders, he decided to check with Yossi whether he had also received the message. He was somewhat surprised to receive a reply in the negative and of course the nature of the question had aroused Yossi's curiosity.

Jack knew he could be facing disciplinary action for failing to contact the station-head first and he emailed back to his colleague,

*'Just some damn-fool Englishman getting kidnapped in Iraq again; do me a favour, forget I even asked.'*

Determined now to play by the book, Jack quickly closed down his computer and marched quickly across to his boss's office.

The small band of information seekers that helped to guard the state of Israel from the plots and machinations of its still quite numerous enemies knew the station head as Ash. His full name was General Asher Giladi. He had arrived in Israel from Iraq in 1949 as a babe in arms. His parents, Shmuel and Hannah had been forced to leave a comfortable middle-class way of life in Baghdad to arrive in Israel as penniless immigrants. Ash had excelled at school and, after the six-day war, had entered the Hebrew University in Jerusalem where he obtained a first class degree in International Affairs. He had decided to make the army a career and the fact that he retired as a general to a senior position in the Mossad spoke eloquently of his ability.

Jack knocked and entered Ash's office to find the station head deeply engrossed in a report. He glanced up and gestured to Jack to take a seat opposite him at the large desk. After just a few moments he closed the file before him and fixed his penetrating gaze on Jack.

'Hello Jack,' Ash began. 'What do you have for me that is so urgent it could not go through channels?'

'Ash,' Jack began, 'please take a look at what I have just emailed to you through the high priority secure channel.'

Even the station head, Ash, was obliged to enter various codes to open files in this channel. After tapping the appropriate keys he started to read what was before him on the screen. Gradually his expression changed from the usual serious attention he always gave to his dispatches. Here was a man who thought he had seen it all. But the more Ash read the more his facial expression changed to one of utter amazement.

'Obviously you have read this carefully?' he demanded, trying valiantly to suppress a look of amused amazement.

'I read it through three times,' Jack replied. 'I could not believe it.'

'Do you think it is a forgery?' Ash enquired with his more usual gravitas taking over.

'I really don't know what to think.' Jack countered. 'If it was from almost anyone other than Sheherezade, I would think it was a joke.'

'They are obviously taking it seriously,' he continued. 'Abdullah Sa'id is a world authority on the period.'

'What is all this stuff about a British soldier?' Ash enquired. 'Civilians are being grabbed all over Iraq but usually it is curtains for any Allied soldier they kidnap. I am going to have to give this investigation top priority. There are too many strange and unanswered questions.'

**Iraq.**
**Leila.**
Craig had now been an unwilling guest in the house for five days. Each morning the Professor would appear after breakfast and spend fifteen or so minutes discussing anything and everything under the sun except the subject that had brought these two men together. Then he would rise to leave and almost as an aside would ask Craig if he now remembered where he had photographed the ancient texts. Craig gave the same answer as he had when he was first brought to the house and the Professor would reply as he left,
'You'll remember, you'll remember.' This was said gently without anger or menace, but Craig was certain that whether he told the Professor about the cave or not, he was more than likely to end up dead. So why give in easily?
Apart from a walk outside in the cool evening air escorted by at least two of the men who had originally captured him, he had plenty of time to think. He thought of his parents, family and friends back in Denton who would now be mourning him. He thought of his girlfriend back home and wished he could tell her how much he loved her. He also thought long and hard about the beautiful girl Leila, the Professor's assistant. She was certainly a devastatingly good-looking girl and he could not help but be aroused sexually just by the thought of her. He would have longed to spend just one night of passionate love with her

and he persuaded himself he would then be able to pledge life long fidelity to the girl back home. But most of all he brooded about the scrolls. The pictures of them had probably saved his life, as without them the terrorists would almost certainly have murdered him and shown a video of the act on the TV screens of the world.

*'What on earth could be written in those scrolls,'* he pondered. *'What could be of such earth-shattering importance?'*

On the sixth morning the Professor did not appear but someone else did, Leila, the girl who created and fuelled his fantasies. She looked just as gorgeous as on their first meeting. British soldiers knew better than to make advances to Iraqi girls. This was a country where such behaviour could quickly result in a sudden and unpleasant death. Craig was certain that his dreams of a passionate affair with Leila would only ever be just that - dreams. He knew he must treat her with respect and caution. In any case she was the enemy wasn't she? This beautiful apparition with her dark hair, olive skin and lithe, but shapely figure was the assistant to the man who was holding him captive.

She locked the door behind her as soon as she entered the room and turned towards him with the sort of smile that almost turned his legs to jelly. At their first meeting she had been pleasant but formal and now she was approaching him as if they were old friends or even old lovers.

'How are you doing?' she enquired. 'You sure are better off here than in that dump where the Professor found you.'

Her English was accented in the slightly guttural and staccato way that Arabic speaking Iraqis speak English, but her choice of phrasing and vocabulary seemed to be more American than English.

'It may be a luxurious prison,' Craig replied, 'but it is still a prison.'

'Do want a Coffee?' she enquired, ignoring his comment.

'No, I'm fine.' Craig replied.' Have one yourself if you want.'

'Look Craig,' Leila continued, 'the Professor is in Baghdad today and has asked me to come and see that you are ok. He also wanted me to ask you a question, but I guess you will know what that question would be.' She finished, smirking slightly.

'Look,' Craig replied somewhat exasperated, 'I've told you people every day now for a week that I don't know or remember exactly where I found those texts. That is what this is all about, isn't it?'

He now felt unexpectedly reckless and decided to try calling his captors bluff. 'Now can I please go back to Basra or are you going to send me back to the thugs who had me before?'

Suddenly a look of alarm crossed Leila's face. 'Shh! Shh!' she said, her long red-tipped index finger to her lips.

Craig looked at her in amazement. What could she have to be secretive or frightened about?

Again she signalled Craig to remain quiet and still while she retraced her steps to the door where she stood motionless, listening for some thirty seconds. Then she was back near the window where Craig was standing.

When she spoke again she spoke loudly and it was in the cold voice that he had heard when they first met.

'I must tell you Craig the Professor is losing patience with you. He is not a violent man but his companions are. We all need to know where the texts were found and if you won't tell us in a friendly way, I guess things are going to become very, very unfriendly.'

Then Leila did the most remarkable thing, she winked at him, gave him a grin, unlocked the door and was gone.

Craig was totally unable to read the situation. One minute she was showing signs of being friendly and the next she was threatening him with dire consequences. What did it all mean? Was she doing the good cop/bad cop routine all rolled into one person? There were lots of questions but no answers.

Nevertheless, the following day, when the door was unlocked at the usual time Craig was more than a little disappointed to find his visitor was the Professor.

This time there were no pleasantries.

'Leila tells me you still won't tell us where you found the texts.' Abdullah stated. 'This has gone on quite long enough. You must know where they were and I am going to give you just one more day to recover your memory. Tomorrow, my friend, you either tell me or I will ask Ali and Mahmoud to persuade you to give the information. 'Why,' he continued, 'are you making such heavy weather out of this? They are just two old texts that need returning to my museum in Baghdad. What is the big secret?'

Craig felt like asking the Professor what was so important about them anyway. Sure they were old. Sure it seemed strange that one should be written in Arabic and the other in Hebrew. Craig knew exactly where he had found them and that seemed to be the key to the whole mystery. That was why he was determined not to tell the Professor. However, whether, or for how long, he could withstand torture became a waking nightmare for the rest of that day. Now there were no fantasies about nights of passion with Leila only a terrible dread about what the two kidnappers would do to him tomorrow

**Jerusalem.**
**At the Highest Level.**

Ash had decided to take Jack with him to Jerusalem. The matter required the highest possible level of security and a need to know basis. Only those who already knew and that meant Jack and Ash, were to be involved.

The two Mossad men were taken to a secure house in the Jerusalem suburb of Talbieh. Here, there were many old style Arab houses built from huge blocks of stone that rendered them cool in summer and warm in winter. However, this type of construction had other advantages. The thickness of the walls rendered the houses almost totally resistant to electronic eavesdropping from the exterior.

The senior officer in charge greeted them warmly. This man, Chaim, was an old friend and colleague of Ash and quite coincidentally had been involved in Jack's training for the security service. Ash and Jack were ushered into a large room and told to wait. The wait seemed incessant, even for men schooled in the art of patience that is so much a part of security training. At first they chatted inconsequentially, but after an hour or more they really did run out of conversation. There was just one subject they did not and could not discuss and that was the reason for their visit to Jerusalem that day. Then eventually, just when Jack had convinced himself that they were on some sort of time-wasting drill, the door to the room opened and a single figure entered. Ash probably knew who they were to see, but to Jack the sight of the Prime Minister came as something of a shock.

Yigal Shomroni had only been in office for some three months. He was the head of a new party that had swept the boards in the election and had achieved an unheard of situation in Israeli politics, an overall majority. He had come to power on the twin planks of security and peace. How that had won him the election when virtually all the other parties had the same policies, could only by explained by his personal charismatic appeal to the voters. Shomroni was tall, very tall. He towered over most of his compatriots. He was also very thin with the athletic figure that he had retained from his younger days as a national basketball hero. He was also religious. Certainly he was no fanatic or bigot but he was a committed member of the Jewish religion. He wore the small knitted skullcap of the modern orthodox Israeli but he had the ability to communicate equally well with the secular population and the religious right. He had dark curly hair, greying at the temples. His face was tanned to a golden brown that seemed to render his light blue, piercing eyes out of place in such a setting. He may have been religious, but to the female voters of Israel he was the glamour boy of Israeli politics. He was however, as later events would show, no team player.

The Prime Minister greeted Ash as an old friend. This was hardly a surprise, as they had known each other since boyhood.

'Ash, my dear fellow,' he began. 'Mah Shlomecha? How are you?'

'Beseder, (ok),' Ash replied.

The contrast between the two men went far beyond the physical. The PM was the classic extrovert where Ash was the typical introverted civil servant.

'Ok,' the PM continued, 'and who is this young man?'

Ash then introduced Jack as one of his team.

'Well Jack, how do you like working for the Mossad?' the PM enquired.

'It is fascinating and very worthwhile work,' Jack quickly answered.

'Ah, an Anglo,' the PM replied recognising Jack's English accented Hebrew and smiling.

'We like Anglos in Israel. You give us more stability.'

Jack grinned. He had heard that many times before. As soon as Israelis recognised his English accent they always seemed to be extra friendly. Coming from a country of football hooligans, binge drinking and violent crime the idea of 'Anglos' giving Israel more stability rather amused him. Still, he hoped, we English Jews have picked up the best, not the worst characteristics of our native land and it is these that the Israelis find so welcoming.

'OK, lets get down to business,' the PM announced with a brusqueness and determination that until now had been hidden by his charm.

'What is this all about my friend?'

The three men walked over to a computer at the far end of the room. Ash keyed in his codes and accessed the long message that had arrived earlier that day from the agent code named Scheherazade.

Shomroni seated himself at the desk and adjusted the seat to allow for his height. He then began to read the email and the more he read the more amazed he became.

Finally he turned to his two companions and said, 'This is dynamite. Who knows about this outside this room?'

'Only Scheherazade and our 'friends' in Iraq,' Ash answered. 'They won't be in any hurry to spread the word. Can you imagine the effect this would have on the Middle East and indeed on the whole world?'

'Hold on,' Shomroni interrupted. 'Who is this British soldier and how much does he know?'

'Scheherazade is not sure. He obviously knows about the existence of the texts because he found them,' Ash answered. 'However,' he continued, 'there is a good chance he does not know what they contain and so far he has resisted all attempts to persuade him to say where he discovered them.'

'If it was anyone other than Abdullah Sa'id holding him the Iraqi terrorists would have tortured the information out of him, and our English friend would be dead by now.' the PM commented. 'As it is I am afraid that poor young man's days are numbered.'

'I am imposing the highest level of security on this whole matter.' the PM continued.

'Only we three and Scheherazade can know of this situation. Now Jack, I need to talk to Ash alone. You are well aware of the high level of secrecy that you must always adopt in your work, but this goes beyond the tightest security you could ever imagine.'

'Just remember that even a single word out of place could cause a civil war to erupt throughout the entire Muslim world that would make the goings-on in Iraq look like a tea-party. These people may not be our friends, but they are our neighbours and if fires are lit all around us, we will also get very badly burned.'

**Return to the Negev.**

After the interview with the Prime Minister the pair had returned to the Mossad station where they were based.

'Jack, go and have a bite in the canteen and then come into my office,' Ash had ordered.

'And Jack,' he added looked desperately serious, 'not one word about this to any of the others.'

In the canteen he had seen Yossi who seemed unusually keen to sit with him while he ate.

'What happened to you today?' Yossi asked. 'Where on earth have you been?'

'Oh, nothing special,' Jack replied, 'I just had to go out to sort one or two things.'

Yossi could see that was all he was going to get out of him and a few minutes later he bade Jack good night.

'Well Jack?' Ash began as soon as he had settled himself in Ash's office. 'I am sure you realise what we are dealing with here. Wrongly handled this information could be the cause of more bloodshed than anything in history and that includes the holocaust. Iran would attack the Saudis and you could guarantee that wherever there are Shi'a Muslims they would attack the Sunnis. You know what is going on in Iraq? Can you imagine that same scenario in just about every Islamic country in the world and worse? Our country could be wiped out and the rest of the Middle East would go up in flames. And that,' he continued, 'would only be for starters.'

'I have no doubt that such a conflagration would involve Europe and the USA. In short we would be dealing with war without end.'

Jack nodded gravely. From the first minute when he had read Scheherazade's message he had realised that they were dealing with something so big that it dwarfed every other situation.

'Jack,' Ash continued, 'you must remain on base this evening. Now leave me please, I have arrangements to make and will call you back later on.'

'Oh just one more thing. I see you have had parachute training. Good! I will let you know where you fit in to our plans in an hour or two.'

Ash bethought himself, 'and Jack, all messages from Scheherazade are now being routed directly to me.'

'I had a date with Dalia tonight in Tel Aviv,' Jack enquired. 'Can I phone her to tell her I won't be able to make it?'

'Yes,' came the reply, 'but just make an excuse and although this is only a personal matter make sure you use a secure line.'

When Jack returned to his desk, most of his colleagues on the day shift had departed for their homes. He took out a book and tried to occupy his mind by reading, but his imagination was racing. Why could he not return home? Ash knew that he was totally discreet and would never compromise the situation. Dalia had been less than happy when he had called to break his date. He had pleaded a touch of Flu and went into some detail to describe how shivery he felt and how much his head hurt. Dalia had offered to come round to his flat and look after him and he had then explained that he had taken ill on the base and would stay there over night. She had then sounded suspicious, but Jack realised that this was probably because she now suspected this whole tale was an excuse. Although they had a good relationship, Dalia would be very jealous if she thought he was involved with another woman. Anyway, if that is what she wanted to think it would have to do for now. *First save the world and then save my relationship*, he smiled ruefully to himself. Dalia was, after all, a very acceptable girlfriend but Jack always knew that in his heart of hearts, the object of his real affections lay elsewhere.

Just half an hour later Jack was summoned again to Ash's office. There he was introduced to Captain Levy of the Israel Air Force Special Commando Unit.

'We're going on a little trip,' Captain Levy told him. .'We should only be away over night but that depends on operational decisions to be made when we arrive. Are you up for this?'

'Yes,' he replied with a grin. Jack had a pretty shrewd idea of where they were heading but in the Mossad you did not ask questions. You just did what was required of you and you gained the information you needed as the operation proceeded.

Three hours later a small, un-marked jet-plane was observed flying low over central, southern Iraq. The allied forces had been notified to give it as much protection as it needed. These orders had come directly from Washington and London and were given the highest level of security clearance. Then in the dark of the Iraqi night three figures could be dimly seen parachuting down from the plane to the desert below.

### A Nocturnal Visitor.

Craig tried to watch the TV in his room until he was bored by the repetition of the CNN and BBC reports of the latest suicide bombs in Baghdad. *Thank heavens Basra is relatively quiet today*, he pondered. However, there was really only one thing on his mind. When would the torture start? He decided to lie down on the bed fully clothed. The chances of him getting any sleep that night were slim and this may well be his last night on Earth. Maybe they would come for him in the dark of night, lead him away, apply the most unimaginable tortures and then when they had broken him, he was sure they would kill him.

It was just after two o'clock in the morning when he thought he heard a sound coming from the hallway. *Oh well, this is it,* he decided. *I won't even be a statistic or a piece of news. In any case, as far as the world knows I am dead already.*

However, there was no further sound until he could have sworn that he heard the key being gently and quietly turned in the lock. He could not imagine any of his kidnappers arriving quietly to take him away to his fate. Jack sat up on the edge of the bed and peered in the dark at the closed door. Then surely and very silently the door began to open and Craig could just make out a shadowy figure gliding into the room. This was no terrorist but a female form and Craig knew that it could only be one person, Leila.

Craig stood up at the side of the bed. The way she had entered the room could only indicate that she did not wish to alert anyone else in the large house to her visit. Suddenly she saw that he was standing up, wide awake and an almost imperceptible whisper emerged from her lips. 'Quiet, please,' she murmured. 'Not a word or we will both be dead.'

It actually crossed Jack's mind at that minute that she must have been attracted to him after all and she was here for a clandestine fulfilment of his own fantasies. Then she spoke again,

'Thank God you are dressed, come on let's go.'

'Go, go where?' Craig demanded, now totally confused.

'Away from here,' she whispered. 'Just follow me.'

The hallway and house were in darkness as they crept down the huge flight of stairs. Leila was carrying a canvas bag that he assumed contained her personal belongings. Across the massive hallway they tiptoed, through the gigantic doorway that had been left ajar and out into the cool desert night.

*Where were the guards?* Craig wondered. Quickly and silently they sped across the open area in front of the house and into the shelter of a few stunted bushes.

Craig was a soldier, a professional well-trained soldier. He was used to danger and in fact prided himself on having nerves of steel. When he heard the voice, however, he almost literally jumped out of his skin.

The word sounded liked 'Po,' repeated quietly and urgently over and over again. Then he saw the three men. They looked like typical Iraqis dressed in navy nylon jackets, checked shirts and jeans. They were talking quietly and earnestly to each other and to his surprise Leila calmly approached them and joined in the conversation.

At first Craig thought they were talking in Arabic but then he realised the accent was even more guttural than Arabic. . It certainly wasn't Farsi, the language of Iran. That sounded totally different. Then one of the men turned to him and smiled.

'Hi Craig,' he said in English. 'Greetings from Israel, consider yourself rescued.'

Then another member of the group gestured urgently for the party to follow him. Swiftly and silently they marched across the open area beyond the shrubs, four men and one girl.

As they walked Craig considered his new situation. These were Israelis who had rescued him. But where did an Iraqi girl like Leila fit in with all this? After all, he realised, she was the one who released him from his captivity and almost certainly saved his life. Why would she have helped him? Even more curious, why would she have helped the Israelis? Had not the Jews and Arabs been sworn enemies for years?

The house and area of his recent imprisonment were now well out of sight some miles behind them. The terrain was typical of the central Iraqi desert with its undulating mounds and low hillocks. The sparseness of the vegetation was to be expected in such a climate and the lack of cover from aerial observation troubled him. However, they were enveloped in wall-to-wall silence disturbed only by the crunching of their boots and trainers on the sandy and rocky terrain.

The Israeli who had spoken to him in English dropped back from his position of third in the line to walk alongside him. Up till then they had been in single file with Leila following immediately behind the leader of the group and this man just behind her.

'Hi Craig,' he addressed the British soldier. 'Are you ok? You have been through some nightmare haven't you?'

'Hi,' Craig answered with a grin. He instantly liked this guy and he spoke such wonderful English. Then the realisation came to him that the guy spoke with a slight Manchester accent.

'What's your name? Are you an Israeli?' he ventured. 'You sound more like a Mancunian to me.'

'Listen Craig,' the man replied in a hushed voice. 'Sure I am Israeli and I can't tell you my name, at least not until you have been debriefed back in Israel. However, I can't hide the fact that I was born and bred in Manchester. It did not take you long to pick up on that,' he finished with a grin.

'Takes one to know one,' Craig retorted grinning back.

'Hey, City or United?' he enquired.

'City, of course,' came the reply.

'Great! You have good taste!'

'I am going to call you 'Blues Supporter' for now. Tell me 'Blues Supporter,' what happened to the guards back at the house and where is the Professor?'

'Look Craig,' the City supporter replied, 'the guards were taken care of by us and that is all I can tell you for now.'

After that short exchange the man resumed his position in the line and silence returned. That was until a hum was heard in the distance. This soon transformed into a much louder sound as a helicopter with US markings came into sight.

The leader of the group began to wave and the helicopter put down in a wide flat area. The group started to run towards the chopper as an American airman jumped out and, bent almost double to avoid the air turbulence caused by the rotor arms of the machine, ran towards them.

'Which of you is Captain Levy?' the American enquired.

'I am,' answered the man who had remained steadfastly at the head of the party during the two-hour march.

'Lieutenant Rogerson of the USAF,' the American replied. 'Boy, are we glad to see you guys!'

'I don't know what the hell you are up to here, but we have been ordered to get you out of Iraq as a priority one.'

With that brief exchange they all climbed into the large helicopter and within minutes they were airborne and flying swiftly into the night. *Two Americans, three Israelis, one British sergeant and an Iraqi girl archaeologist; what a strange crew?* Craig pondered.

**Amman. Jordan.**

They had been flying for just over an hour when Lieutenant Rogerson announced that they were now in Jordanian airspace. Soon after that, they landed and the party of five disembarked. Craig was astonished to see vehicles with the markings of the Royal Jordanian Army parked on the perimeter of the airstrip. A large people carrier was waiting for them and they were quickly whisked away in it to a large white villa on the edge of the city of Amman. Here they were each offered clean clothing and separate rooms to enjoy a few hours rest. Craig only then realised that he was totally exhausted and was in a deep sleep as soon as his head hit the pillow.

He was disturbed some three hours later by the bedside telephone summoning him to a meeting room on the same floor. Craig showered and dressed quickly in the jeans and cotton shirt provided by his hosts and joined the others. There was no sign of Captain Levy or the other Israeli but Leila and 'Blues Supporter' were there together with a smartly dressed middle age man who Craig correctly assumed to be a Jordanian.

The Jordanian greeted him in perfect Oxford English and asked him to sit beside him at the long table. Leila and 'Blues Supporter' were sitting opposite. That suited Craig very well. Despite his ordeal he could still derive considerable pleasure just from looking at that lovely face.

'My name is Prince Jamal ibn Musa, third cousin of his Majesty the King,' the Jordanian began with more than a degree of pomposity.

Craig was not a little impressed. Here was he a British Sergeant in the company of a member of the Jordanian Royal family. However, what he really wanted above all was to contact his family in Manchester to tell them the great news that he was alive, well and free from captivity.

Craig made to rise to show due deference to the man he now realised to be his host. However, the Prince signalled him to remain seated and the conversation continued.

'I understand from my friend Yigal Shomroni the Prime Minister of Israel, that you have something to show me,' he said addressing Leila.

'Yes sir,' she replied and placed the bag she had brought with her from Iraq on the table. Rising to look inside she produced a CD.'

She crossed the floor and they all stared at the huge plasma screen as the data was loaded into the drive of the computer sitting alongside it.

*So that is what this is all about*, mused Craig as the photograph he had taken of the Arabic scroll appeared.

'And now Sergeant,' the Prince said after studying the photographs of both of the texts that Craig had taken, 'I believe you found these texts and took these photos. Can you please tell me where you found them.'

Here we go again thought Craig. What on earth can be in the scrolls? First they got me away from the Iraqi kidnappers to be imprisoned again by the Professor. Then they seemed to bring the Israelis into the picture. Then, with some American help, they rescued me from Iraq. Now a Jordanian Prince is in the frame and he is talking about having discussed the texts with the Prime Minister of Israel.

'Sir,' Craig found himself saying. 'I am more than grateful to you all for getting me away from a certain death in Iraq, but I found the texts. I am on active service in Iraq, as you all know, as a member of the British Army. I think that the information of where I found them can only be turned over by me to my Commanding Officer in Basra.'

His companions looked at him with incredulity. Here was this British sergeant, officially dead and who had just been rescued from a horrible fate and he was insisting on what he deemed to be the correct protocol in dealing with the texts.

The Prince looked mildly irritated.

'Sergeant, first of all you can not be on active service in Iraq if you are in Jordan and as far as your regiment is concerned you are dead and buried. What is the problem with telling us where they were found?'

The Prince continued with not a little sarcasm. 'They are written in Arabic and Hebrew and that tends to indicate, don't you think, that they must belong to the Arab and Jewish people, not to our good friends the British?'

'Yes Sir,' Craig could hardly believe what he was saying himself. 'But I take my orders from my Commanding Officers not from anyone else - friends as I know you all are both to me and to my country.'

The Prince turned with a look of utter exasperation to Leila and the man Craig still called 'Blues Supporter.'

'Maybe you can do something to get this guy to see sense.'

'Sir,' Leila suggested, 'perhaps I could have a private word with the Sergeant.'

'Of course,' said the Prince and the two men left the room to leave Craig alone with this beautiful woman.

'Now Craig, I know I asked you before to tell me where you found the texts but then you thought I was part of the enemy. Craig,' she continued, 'I am going to tell you who I really am and that is a secret in my world known to probably no more than six other people.'

'My name is Leila, Leila Hasdai! I was born in Iraq into an ancient Iraqi Jewish family who could trace their roots back to long before the country was conquered by the Muslims.'

'However, after the 1973 war between Israel and the Arabs the position became totally impossible for my family there. I was a baby in arms and we were more than lucky to be able to escape. We went to America where I was educated. Our family name was changed to Harris and I eventually decided to write a thesis at UCLA on the Caliphate of Baghdad.'

'Ok,' Craig interrupted with a faint smile. 'That explains a lot.'

'It was there that I met Professor Abdullah Sa'id,' she continued. 'He took me under his wing and I made up a story about being an Iraqi Muslim. I knew he would never be able to trust me as a Jew.'

'He wished to continue his research back in Iraq once Sadam Hussein had been removed from power and asked me to accompany him. He saw that all the formalities and arrangements were completed to leave the USA.'

'Ok,' said Craig again, 'so then what happened?'

'The night before we left I had a visit from General Ash Giladi of the Israel Secret Service. He knew my family history even better than I did and I allowed myself to be persuaded to give reports of events in Iraq to the Mossad.'

'I did pass the Israelis lots of good information, but nothing sensational - at least not until you arrived on the scene with your two photographs.'

'The two scrolls! The two scrolls! What on earth is in the two scrolls that is upsetting everyone so much?' Jack enquired.

'Ah, so the texts were in scrolls,' Leila replied. 'At least that is one new piece of information you have given us.'

Craig looked momentarily uncomfortable and then realised that old texts such as these could only have been preserved if in scroll form anyway.

'I cannot give you an explanation at the moment,' she continued, 'but I promise you that as soon as we can, you will be told. However, you will be given the information only under terms of strict secrecy. When I tell you the contents you will understand why the situation is so delicate.'

Leila continued, 'your fellow Mancunian is called Jack. As soon as you tell us where the scrolls were found he will escort you over the river Jordan to Israel and from there you can be flown back to England to be reunited with your friends and family at home.'

Needless to say Craig still refused to supply the information. He was grateful that she had not tried to seduce him in to giving her the information and he wondered whether he would have succumbed if she had chosen that route.

Leila, for her part, was a lady who was very much in control but she could feel the anger rising in her as she left Craig alone in the room and went to report to the others. So it was decided that Jack would try to persuade Craig to give him the information. They discussed football at some length, Manchester and places familiar to them both in their youth, but still Craig remained silent. The Prince and Leila then returned to the room and the Prince again spoke to Craig.

'Look Sergeant, I am a Sandhurst man myself and I very much respect your loyalty to the regiment and the British army. However, can't you see you are among friends here?'

'Of course I can, Sir,' Craig replied obligingly, 'but I cannot divulge information to foreign nationals, even friendly ones without permission of my C.O.'

The Prince sat quietly pondering the situation.

'All right Craig,' he said 'How would it be if I asked the British Ambassador to Jordan to come here and you gave him the information?'

Craig could at last see a way out of the impasse.

'Yes Sir,' he replied, 'that would be fine.'

As it transpired the Ambassador had been back to London for consultation with the Foreign Office but he was due to return the following day. Jack took his leave and prepared to report back to Ash in Israel. Leila it was decided, would remain in the safe house outside Amman until Craig had passed on the details of the location of the scrolls to the British Ambassador. Then she would be returned to Iraq with a suitable cover story of a trip the previous day and night to Baghdad to cover her absence. And the Prince, after ensuring the comfort of his guests, prepared to leave. As for the photographs, they were already saved on the hard drive of the high security PC that was accessible only to the Prime Minister of Israel and now they were also saved on the private computer of the Jordanian Prince. That having been achieved, the CD Leila had brought from Iraq was destroyed. However, Craig's mobile cell phone was still in the hands of Professor Sa'id.

The danger of the story being leaked to an unsuspecting world was growing. Most of the people who were aware of the existence of the ancient documents were totally reliable and had nothing to gain and almost a world to lose if the news of the existence of the two texts became public. However, what had begun with Craig photographing the texts had now brought the knowledge of the existence of the scrolls to four fanatical Sunni insurgents, an Iraqi Professor, an undercover Israeli girl secret agent, the spymaster of the Mossad, an Anglo-Israeli Mossad operative, the Prime Minister of Israel and a Royal Prince of Jordan. All of these people had read and understood the document, in one language or the other and had realised the terrible implications that could arise from publication. The only person who had no idea of the substance of the texts was the man who originally found them, Sergeant Craig Blackburn.

## The Rev. Bill Cooper

By late afternoon Jack was back at his desk in the Negev. He reported to Ash on the relative success of the mission. He told him of the determination of Sergeant Craig Blackburn not to divulge the origin of the scrolls, but otherwise Ash was reasonably satisfied with Jack's news.

'Are you sure the Jordanians won't persuade Sergeant Blackburn to divulge the location of the scrolls?' Ash wanted to know. 'Between you and me, I was horrified when I discovered that our Prime Minister had involved Jordan. I really do not understand why he did this.'

'Prince Jamal is terrified of the effect that a leak of the contents would have on his country,' Jack assured him. 'He is the only man in Jordan who has seen the texts or even knows of their existence. At the moment he is taking a considerable personal risk in withholding the information from the King and the Jordanian Prime Minister. I have to say that this also seems very strange behaviour.'

'Short of torture, and that certainly does not seem to be the Prince's style, he would never be able to get the information out of Craig Blackburn,' Jack continued. 'I have to say that even if by some miracle Craig decided to confide in him, the Prince would be insane to try to go it alone in Iraq to steal or destroy the scrolls. Remember we all have emails of the photographs of the texts and so does Professor Sa'id.'

There was just one other person who suspected that something very important was going on. He had watched with great interest the comings and goings of Ash and Jack. He had become suspicious that something was afoot by the way that Jack had tried to cover up his initial amazement at the original signal from Sheherezade.

Yossi Sharoni was a good Mossad operative. He was loyal to the organisation to which he had pledged his allegiance and he loved his country and its people. All Mossad operatives are psychologically profiled on a regular basis. Any hint of excessive fanaticism whether political or religious was frowned upon. They were there to do a job with military precision and without emotion. Yossi was not particularly religious and that was in his favour. He was however, unbeknown to the Mossad, seriously compromised.

He had recently been sent on a trip to the USA where he had received instructions to build a relationship with the Rev. Bill Cooper, a right wing Christian and a great friend of Israel. The Rev. Cooper, in common with many Bible belt Americans, was convinced that to achieve the Second Coming of Jesus, the Jews must be strong and settled in the Holy Land. He therefore saw all Muslims as the enemy and did everything in his power to reverse what he saw as the Islamic threat to what he called the entire Judeo-Christian world.

Every day Yossi saw the results of the fanaticism induced by the preaching of religious hatred - Islamic suicide bombs. He was also aware of the occasional manifestation of terrorism among his own people. That had culminated in the assassination of Yitzchak Rabin, Prime Minister of Israel, by a misguided Jewish zealot. It was therefore amazing that a down-to-earth pragmatist like Yossi could come under the influence of the Rev. Bill Cooper of the Church of the Second Coming. However, that is exactly what had happened.

Yossi had looked forward to his visit to the USA. He was also interested in what made so many American Protestants into such strong and loyal supporters of Israel. Rev. Bill, as his many thousands of followers knew him, was also looking forward to the visit of a known Mossad operative. He always hoped for fanatical support for their country from Israelis and had been disappointed that so few of the ones he had met could accept his Messianic view of the future. Yossi's brief was to organise and discuss the security aspects of a forthcoming visit to Israel by Rev. Bill. Those discussions had proceeded well and, with all the security business concluded, Rev. Bill invited Yossi to attend one of his meetings. This was to take place in a huge arena in Dallas and, with nothing else to do, Yossi agreed to accompany his new friend. Deep down he felt uncomfortable accepting this invitation, but a combination of curiosity and not wishing to offend enabled him to persuade himself to accept.

The Rev. Bill Cooper was over six feet in height. He had the lean, but powerful build of a football or rugby player that belied his sixty-two years. His classic handsome Nordic features were invariably tanned to a rich golden brown be it winter or summer. To perfect the image of a

Southern preacher he sported a snow-white goatee beard. His equally white hair, immaculately coiffed, was neatly cut to rest just below the collar of his white shirt. His deep voice resonated with a strong southern drawl. It would have come as a considerable shock to the many thousands who followed him and even to his family and closest associates if they had discovered that he was neither a Baptist, nor a Christian, nor a Southerner.

His father had arrived in New York from the Ukraine in the early nineteen thirties with the name Hymie Cohen. He had quickly decided that this name sounded more like a Jewish joke than a real name and quickly adopted the name of Harold Cooper.

Harold Cooper, or rather Hymie Cohen, had been determined to escape from the Ukraine with its endemic anti-Semitism. He had also wanted to escape from his family and the religion that he considered to be stifling and restrictive. Harold Cooper quickly made his way in the new country as a small time timber merchant' salesman. He had then started his own timber business and it was not long before he met Greta Sorensen, an attractive Swedish immigrant. She too had arrived in the USA determined to make her way in whatever profession would give her the fastest route to wealth. For a short time she had earned her daily bread as a nightclub hostess and had then persuaded some of the other girls to join her in an enterprise that was really no more and no less than a bordello. Between them the couple had amassed a small fortune by the end of the war catering for the needs of the military, the business community and government members. They had then decided to start a family. They had one son William who, after graduating from college, had quickly realised that with a good education one of the finest ways of extracting money from a gullible American public was by playing on their religious sensibilities. And so, with a move to Arkansas the Rev Bill Cooper was born. He had been an accomplished actor at school and quickly perfected his southern drawl.

The motorcade bearing the Rev. Bill and Yossi pulled up at the side entrance to the arena and Yossi was professionally impressed to see a number of security men jump out of the cars following them and carefully and alertly usher Bill and Yossi into a luxurious dressing room inside the building. Bill had been wearing an immaculately tailored light cream coloured suit, but this was quickly discarded in favour of a frock coat with a waistcoat and narrow ribbon tie of the type worn by confederate officers, over two centuries earlier.

A series of visitors then arrived. Rev. Bill greeted them all with considerable warmth. He lost no time in introducing Yossi as a visitor from Israel. He confided in his loud southern drawl that Yossi had an important job with the Israeli government. This went down very well with Bill's associates who all tried to enter into long and detailed discussions about the political situation at home. Yossi was both flattered and a little uncomfortable as he tried to avoid imparting any sensitive information in answer to the probing questions of these people.

Eventually the time arrived for the Rev. Bill and his party to make their way to the huge stage. Yossi emerged from the wings accompanied by a number of the senior churchmen and he was flattered to see that his name card was attached to a seat next to that reserved for the Rev. Bill. He really was getting star treatment. Once the party was all settled there was a drum roll and the Rev. Bill marched on to the stage. As he made his way to his seat the huge audience rose to its feet and applauded and waved enthusiastically. The noise was deafening. However, as soon as the Rev. Bill raised his arms the entire assembly fell silent and resumed their seats.

Then the Rev. Bill started to speak. His speech was full of anger and passion.

'May God bless you all,' he intoned. 'You people are the pride of our great country. You have made America the greatest country on earth and with the help of the Almighty we will vanquish the foes within and the foes without. Let us now pray together as the mighty multitude that we are.

'Holy Father, please empower us to cleanse the world of all the evil we see around us. Help us to prepare the way for the return of your only son, Lord Jesus Christ. Send abundant blessings on his people, the people of Israel to make them strong in their land and to vanquish all their enemies.'

As he spoke his tone became more and more strident and his followers began to cheer and applaud wildly with each and every statement.

'Oh Lord, help us to destroy the curses of pornography and obscenity which poison our great land.'

'Oh Lord, help us to show our Christian brothers that only a pure faith such as ours, uncluttered by the pomp of Archbishops, Bishops and yes, Popes, can bring real salvation.'

'Oh Lord, help us to show the misguided adherents of Islam that their path will lead them to damnation and not to the paradise they seek.'

This impassioned flow continued for the best part of an hour, by which time his followers were hoarse from cheering, but buoyed on by the emotions the Rev. Bill had built up in them.

Then suddenly he gestured to the huge audience to resume their seats and in quiet measured tones he told them that today they were honoured to have in their midst a representative of the Israeli government.

Yossi wondered who that might be and looked round the assembly for a likely candidate for that description. Then he heard the Rev. Bill announce, 'My dear friends please give a warm welcome to Yossi Sharoni.'

Yossi was horrified. He realised that he was being used and that he should never have accepted Bill's invitation to accompany him. There were thousands of people here and there could well be a sprinkling of spies from organisations antithetical to Bill's. These could undoubtedly include members of Islamic groups who saw the Rev. Bill Cooper and everything he stood for as a threat to them. He was sure his cover was blown wide open and he was convinced that the usual gaggle of media people would already be contacting their papers, TV and radio stations to check out whom this Yossi Sharoni really was.

All these thoughts were bouncing around in his head as he dimly heard Rev. Bill saying,

'So Yossi, will you say a few words to all my wonderful friends, gathered here today?'

As he rose somewhat hesitantly to his feet, Yossi was certain that once his boss Ash Giladi heard of this debacle he would be looking for a new job and definitely not working for any department of the Government of Israel. Thinking on the move was something every Mossad operative was trained to do. However, public speaking to thousands of hyped up American Christians was not part of any training he had ever undertaken. Still he had to say something and, rising to his feet, he issued just a few bland words to cover the situation.

'Hello my friends,' he began. 'May I thank you, Rev. Bill for asking me to speak. I would just like to say that I bring the greetings of the people of Israel to the people of America. May I thank you all for your support for us through all the difficulties that we have to contend with.'

Yossi then resumed his seat and was astonished to realise that his simple greeting had produced a similar level of applause to that given to his host's long and passionate speech.

Then Rev. Bill was up on his feet again.

'You all know who we have to support don't you? Israel! It is only by supporting Israel that we can hasten the second coming. God bless Israel!'

The crowd immediately started to chant 'God Bless Israel!' which should have made Yossi feel very happy, but instead made him feel very, very uncomfortable.

**Amman.**
Her Britannic Majesty's Ambassador to the Hashemite Kingdom of Jordan was George Carmichael. He was a young career diplomat who had previously served in senior positions in the British embassies in Cairo and Kuwait. He spoke fluent Arabic and excellent French and in the foreign office he was tipped for the top position of Ambassador to Washington in the not too far distant future.

Carmichael had decided to interview Craig Blackburn in the Embassy, after being briefed about the missing scrolls in a secret meeting with Prince Jamal. Although the British, quite justifiably, looked upon the Hashemite Kingdom of the Jordan as good friends, there was something about the demeanour of this Royal Prince that worried the Ambassador. Carmichael had known Prince Jamal for some time, but he sensed some uncharacteristic inner turmoil at the meeting. Possibly the fact that no other member of the Royal Family or the Jordanian Government had been informed by the Prince was what added to the Ambassador's concern.

'Look here, old boy,' the Prince had told him with his unmistakeable English Public School accent, 'the Israeli PM told me about the scrolls and I feel that for now the less people in the know about them, the better.'

*Of course,* Carmichael pondered, *that was quite correct as far as it went. However, the Prince was implying a lack of reliability in members of his own family, no doubt including the King. This also included the Prime Minister and other senior members of the Jordanian Cabinet.* The Ambassador was uncomfortable.

Craig, on the other hand, was delighted to be transferred to the Embassy. He had been very concerned about the prospect of discussing his find in the presence of anyone who was not a representative of either the British government or military and he had been sure that both the Prince and the Israelis would have been present if he was to be interviewed at his present location.

Prince Jamal ibn Mussa, on the other hand, was far from pleased. He had only been involved in the affair as a result of a hasty decision taken by Yigal Shomroni, the impulsive new Israeli Prime Minister. Having seen the text of the scrolls or at least the Hebrew one, he felt he must have an ally in the Arab world. The ally must be from a country already having relatively good relations with Israel and with Great Britain. Even more importantly he must be a senior government member of a moderate Sunni Muslim country as they had everything to gain and nothing to lose from the permanent suppression of the existence of this declaration from the past. So, without consultation even with the Mossad, Shomroni had contacted Jamal ibn Mussa. Shomroni knew the Prince very well and they had been close friends since the days when both men had been members of their respective delegations at peace conferences between their two countries.

The Mossad, in the person of Asher Giladi, was deeply shocked when the Prime Minister told him what he had done. It took all of his, not inconsiderable, powers of self-control to refrain from informing the PM of the terrible risk he was taking in involving Jordan in the secret. However, Ash held his tongue, but suggested that as Jordan, or rather one Jordanian Prince, was now a party to the conspiracy, they could be made use of as a half way house between Israel and Iraq. That way the British soldier Craig Blackburn could be questioned there, which would be less compromising for Israeli security. Now it transpired that the British soldier was to be removed from Jordanian jurisdiction and taken to the Embassy. That was certainly not what either the Prince or the Israelis had intended, but they could not offend the British by refusing to release the soldier.

An Embassy car collected Craig from the house and drove him to the meeting with the Ambassador. Craig quickly spotted that British and Jordanian security men were escorting them. He knew that even Amman had not been spared the attention of terrorists including suicide bombers, obviously as a spill over of events in neighbouring Iraq. Craig was used to danger, but here in a busy and apparently normal city he felt more nervous than in Iraq where tried and tested security measures were permanently in place.

After being ushered through a number of security checks he was invited to enter the private office of the Ambassador. There, George Carmichael was waiting for him. Craig took an instant liking to the Ambassador. He expected some middle-aged public-school type who would talk down to him and the young Scotsman who faced him, with his soft lowlands accent, was certainly a very pleasant and unexpected surprise.

'So you are Sergeant Blackburn,' the Ambassador began. Then with a grin he continued, 'I don't know what you are doing here. According to London you are supposed to be dead!'

'I suspected as much, Sir,' Craig replied.

'Look Craig, at the moment you are an 'un-person' and I therefore think we can dispense with the Ambassador and Sergeant routine. My name is George, so just call me that.'

'Certainly Sir, I mean George,' Craig replied.

'Right, now can we get down to working out what all the fuss is about. The Israelis and some Iraqis have all been using unofficial channels to try and get more information about whatever it is you found.'

At last, Craig realised, he could safely tell the whole story to someone clearly entitled to receive the information. Craig sadly recounted to the Ambassador the full story of how his friends had been killed, how he had found the two scrolls and the importance Professor Sa'id and the Mossad together with Prince Jamal, accorded to persuading him to provide the location of his discovery.

The Ambassador listened in silence and only when Craig had finished the long and somewhat convoluted story did he speak.

'Ok, Craig,' George replied, 'but the one thing you have not told me is what is written in these scrolls.'

'That is the problem,' Craig replied, 'everyone but me seems to know, but I can't read either Arabic or Hebrew and I don't have the slightest idea.'

'Where are the photographs of the texts?' George Carmichael then enquired.

'All I know is that they are on the disk of the computer of Professor Sa'id in Iraq and saved on the computer of Prince Jamal. As for my phone, my guess is that Abdullah Sa'id would have erased the pictures as soon as he had downloaded them on to his machine.'

'How about the Israelis?' the Ambassador then enquired.

'I am sure they have them,' Craig responded. 'Leila must have somehow emailed them from Iraq to Israel before they brought me out.'

The Ambassador thought for a moment.

'This whole situation is very strange. The Iraqi Professor, the Jordanians and Israel are going to considerable trouble to try and discover the whereabouts of the original scrolls. You said they are in a cave in the middle of the desert, didn't you?' Craig nodded.

'There is also a total silence from all three parties as to what these texts contain.'

The Ambassador was addressing Craig, but he was also thinking aloud as he tried to find a reason to why three such disparate groups should have exciting information about apparently ancient texts and be going to such considerable lengths to keep it secret from virtually the rest of the world.

'When Prince Jamal asked me to see you,' George continued. 'He told me that you had found and photographed two old texts and refused to say where the originals were located. Now I know the answer to that question, but I cannot pass the information on without consulting the Foreign Office. They will probably involve our security people. The Prince is just going to have to accept that for the time being.'

There was a lull in the conversation while George Carmichael considered the strange situation in which they had been placed. Craig decided that now was the time to re-open the matter of his own status. He desperately needed to notify his family that he was alive and well.

'George,' he began tentatively, 'I have told you everything I know. Please now may I phone my parents.'

The Ambassador gave him a searching look. Up till now he had seemed warm, friendly and considerate.

'I am afraid I cannot sanction that,' George replied coldly. 'You must understand that I am answerable to the Foreign Office and they will not agree, without the sanction of the Security Service, to you breaking the cover you have inadvertently established for yourself. I will send off a signal to London giving all the details of our meeting and ask them what the situation is for you to contact your family.'

'In the meantime I must inform you,' the Ambassador continued, 'that you are under strict orders not to contact anyone. Not your family and certainly neither the Jordanians nor the Israelis.'

'I suggest you make yourself at home here in the Embassy until I receive further instructions.'

Craig was deeply disappointed. He had been a prisoner of terrorists, then of Professor Sa'id, then Prince Jamal and now he was virtually a prisoner of his own people, the British.

'What harm would it do?' he ventured, 'to phone my parents and tell them I am alive and well, but in a secret location.'

'Sorry,' came the reply. 'No can do! Make yourself comfortable. There are magazines in the cupboard and the TV has lots of English programmes. I will be back as soon as I have a reply from London.'

Craig tried to read and then tried the TV. He flicked through dozens of stations, but nothing held his attention. Eventually a Jordanian servant at the Embassy brought him a delicious meal, but he was too upset to eat much of it.

After a while the Ambassador returned to say he had reported everything to the Foreign Office and did not expect a reply before the following morning. He was allocated a very comfortable room, but all Craig yearned for was his small room in the family house in Denton with its football posters and pin-ups.

**El Paso.**

The next stop on the Rev. Bill's tour was in El Paso and it was only there, some hours later that Yossi was able to speak privately to his host.

They were in a large house on the edge of the town and surrounded by a comforting array of security features. From what Yossi could see, no unauthorised person could enter the grounds of the villa, let alone the house itself. As a professional he knew there was no such thing as total security, but this looked like a state-of-the-art installation.

'I do wish you had not asked me to address your supporters,' he ventured, once they were alone. 'You know my role is security and my cover is now blown wide open.'

'I don't think so,' the Rev. Bill replied. 'You were among friends in Dallas and you can report that back to your boss in Israel when you fly home tomorrow.'

'If I tell him what happened I will be fired on the spot,' Yossi tried to explain.

'Do you think we allow just anyone into our meetings?' Bill commented, ignoring Yossi's comment.

'Every one of those people in the audience was there by invitation and screened by my security men before being admitted. We are not total idiots here you know.' He finished, sounding a little irritated.

'Anyway, you don't need to come to the El Paso meeting. Just stay here and chill out.'

Yossi settled himself down in the suite that had been allocated to him and started to enjoy the dinner that had mysteriously arrived soon after the departure of his host. He never drank on duty and in fact rarely indulged in alcohol except for the occasional glass of white wine. However, a bottle of one of the best Golan wines accompanied the meal and in the knowledge that he could sleep off the effects by morning he slowly sipped his way through the entire bottle. Eventually, and feeling a little giddy, he decided to take a shower and prepare for bed. The shower did little to sober him up and wearing just the towelling robe he had discovered in the bathroom, he made for the huge plasma TV screen to relax a little more before retiring to bed.

Yossi must have dozed off in the comfortable armchair because he was awakened by a knock at the room door.

*Who the hell is this,* he brooded as he strolled over to peep through the spy hole to see who was there. Then he remembered that the door was monitored by CCTV and looked up at the screen to see whom it could be that was disturbing him. Outside in the corridor stood a young woman of somewhat severe appearance.

'Hello?' Yossi enquired through the microphone, 'I think you have the wrong room.'

'Are you Yossi Sharoni?' the female voice enquired.

'Yes,' Yossi repeated. 'What do you want?'

'I am Jilly, PA to Rev. Cooper. Can I please come in to check over one or two details with you?'

The woman certainly did not look like a security threat and in any case Yossi's reactions were somewhat dulled by the amount of wine he had consumed. He pressed the button to release the door and the woman entered.

She was about five feet five inches in height and was wearing a somewhat shapeless, fine tweed dress with long sleeves. It was zipped right up to her neck to ensure that the only flesh showing was her face and hands. She had what looked like natural blonde hair scooped back into a bun and her only contribution to cosmetics was in highlighting her rather piercing blue eyes. The woman wore old-fashioned plastic framed spectacles and her feet were encased in flat walking shoes. She was probably about thirty years old, but the way she was dressed made this hard to ascertain.

'Hi, I am Jilly,' she repeated. 'Can I sit down for a minute?'

'Sure,' Yossi replied. This woman's appearance puzzled him. She was dressed in the same modest manner as most of the women he had seen at the Dallas meeting. However, her eyes, or rather the way she looked at him, troubled him.

'Anyway,' Yossi continued. 'I am rather tired. What can I do for you?'

'Of course,' the woman replied glancing meaningfully at the empty wine bottle.

'The Rev. Cooper just wanted to be sure that you have everything you need.'

'So,' she continued conversationally. 'Have you enjoyed your trip to the USA?'

She seemed to want to chat and Yossi who was not averse to women's company was quite pleased to oblige. Deep down he hoped that she would not realise that he was a little drunk and he was determined to concentrate on the inconsequential conversation on which they were embarking.

Yossi liked her voice. Somehow it did not fit her appearance. It was too sexy by far, he decided, for a frumpy religious woman.

After a few minutes Yossi felt the need to visit the bathroom and excused himself. When he returned he was surprised to see that Jilly had released her hair and that it now cascaded down the sides of her face. Also he quickly noticed that she had zipped down her dress to reveal a long and shapely neck and just a modest amount of cleavage.

Yossi returned to his armchair opposite where Jilly was sitting and in his still somewhat bemused state sat gazing in astonishment at the minor changes in her appearance that had suddenly transformed her into a far more desirable example of American womanhood.

'Enjoying the view?' Jilly enquired, grinning as she removed her glasses.

'Oh sorry!' Yossi replied. 'I did not mean to stare, but you look so different from a few moments ago.'

'In what way?' she enquired impishly.

Yossi stammered. He did not know what to say. He was used to secular Israeli women who were often as sexually aggressive as the men. He had no experience of religious women and when their paths crossed either at work or socially, he always treated them with great respect. Now here was an obviously religious woman from a Christian organisation with whom he was supposed to be working, who seemed to be teasing or tempting him. Suddenly he realised that he was only wearing the towelling bathrobe and he subconsciously wrapped it further round him and tightened the cord.

'I just thought you looked different with your hair down,' he stuttered.

'I see you have a mini-bar,' she enquired after a short pause. 'You seem to be at least five drinks ahead of me. Do you think you could find me a Vodka and tonic in there?'

'I thought you people did not drink?' Yossi replied a little rudely.

'What we do in public and what we do in private are not necessarily the same thing.' She replied, grinning and staring at him in a way that made him feel that she was imagining him stark naked.

Yossi rose from the chair and crossed the room to find the required vodka and tonic for his guest. As he poured out the drink with his back to her, he realised that she had also crossed the room and was standing silently behind him. He turned to give her the drink and could see that the long zip was now fully open and beneath it she was wearing absolutely nothing.

'Hello,' she said in a husky voice. 'Are you enjoying the view?'

Yossi was convinced that this situation could not be right and had he been sober he would undoubtedly have controlled the desire welling up inside him and asked her to leave. However, instead he took the glass back from her that he had just prepared and taking her hands in his, he gently pulled her towards him. It took only another minute for them to be lying naked, their bodies interlocked, on the huge double bed in which he had so much wanted just to sleep.

**Amman.**

The Prince Jamal waited all day for a phone call from the British Ambassador. When it arrived he was more than a little disappointed. *Still,* he contemplated, *the important thing, at this stage, was to keep the information away from those who would use it to cause trouble. The British may now know where the scrolls were to be found, but they still had no idea what was written in them.* He, on the other hand knew exactly what was inscribed on the ancient parchments and the mere thought of what he could do with that information made him physically tremble.

Leila, in the meantime, had returned to Baghdad from where she was assured by the Americans that reliable Iraqi police officers would see her safely returned to the house of Professor Sa'id. For her to stay away for any longer period would have aroused her employer's suspicions. Two unmarked, but heavily armed police cars were used to take her back, but she was met on her arrival by a scene of utter devastation. The large and beautiful house was just a smoking ruin. It was impossible to contact Israel in the presence of the Iraqi police and she was anxious to know the fate of Professor Sa'id and whether any evidence of the existence of the scrolls had been recovered from the fire. She returned to Baghdad and registered in the Al Mansour Hotel, within the secure compound where foreign visitors, journalists and senior Iraqi officials were to be found. She then had to get a signal out to her boss Ash Giladi in Israel.

The Al Mansour was popular with the senior members of the International Press Corp. Apart from being comfortably furnished to the highest standards of the day every room was fitted with a state of the art computer system. This facilitated the transmission of the latest information from this tragic country to all parts of the world. Leila had decided that with so much activity emanating in cyber space from this hotel she could afford to send coded messages from her room. This would normally have been unthinkable, but the news of the destruction of the house and the disappearance of its owner must be sent to Israel without delay. In a city of daily bomb blasts and the resultant tragically high death toll, the news of a fire destroying the large and palatial desert home of a Professor of archaeology was of little interest. Had it not been for the disappearance of Professor Sa'id himself, it would probably not have rated a mention. However, he was one of the academics in Baghdad who was of international renown.

Leila sent her coded email to Yusuf, another Israeli agent in Iraq. From there her message was forwarded to the Mossad operative based in Nicosia, Cyprus. Only then could the message arrive in the Negev base, still in coded form, to be opened and decoded by Ash Giladi. Once the message reporting on the news was transmitted Leila set about removing the hard disk from the computer. Even if the message was deleted there was still the possibility that a determined official, sufficiently capable in such matters, would have been able to restore the deleted message.

Decoding it was another matter, but the authorities would have been very suspicious indeed as to why the assistant of the missing Professor Sa'id would have been sending out coded messages in the first place. The next problem was how and where to dispose of the disk. She had just placed it in her handbag when there was a knock on the door of her room. There were three visitors, two Iraqi plain-clothes policemen and an American Lieutenant.

After the usual greetings were exchanged, the senior Iraqi policeman raised the subject of their visit. He looked most uncomfortable as he addressed her in Arabic.

'We are sorry to disturb you Ms Harris, but we know from our colleagues that they took you out to the house of Professor Sa'id today and that neither you nor they were aware that the house had burned down early this morning.'

'I need to ask you a few questions as we are very worried, as I am sure you are, for the safety of the Professor.'

The Iraqi then switched to a very passable American English and continued,

'Before I proceed may I introduce Lieutenant Johnson who is present to protect your interests as an American subject.'

The American grinned and said, 'Hi!'

'Hi to you,' Leila replied aware as ever of the effect she had on most men when they first met her. She was not a vain person, but she had known since her mid-teens that most members of the male species found her extremely attractive.

'So Inspector,' she said, addressing the Iraqi in Arabic. 'What do you think has happened to Professor Sa'id?'

'With respect Ms Harris, it is I who must ask you questions not the other way round.'

'Of course,' Leila answered smiling. 'But please understand I have worked for some years with the Professor and naturally I worry on a personal basis for his safety.'

It was the Iraqi Inspector's turn to say, 'Of course.'

'Now, Ms Harris,' he continued. 'Please can you account for your movements for the last two days?'

Leila had her story ready. She had driven overnight, on her own, to Baghdad where she wished to undertake some research for the Professor into recently discovered documents from the time of the Caliph An-Nasir. *This was dangerously near the truth, but talk of old documents without political or religious significance would be of no interest to the police.* Then, she explained, she had decided to take a twenty-four hour break at her own apartment in the residential and relatively peaceful suburb of Mansour just outside the main city area and not far from this hotel. However, she explained, she had realised that to return to the Professor's house in the desert in broad daylight, on her own, was foolhardy and she had requested a police escort through the good offices of American friends. She was after all, she reminded them, an American citizen. However, when she saw the burned out wreckage of where she was supposed to work she was frightened to return to her home alone and the police escort had kindly brought her back to this hotel.

'So you have no idea of what can have happened to the Professor?' the Inspector enquired again.

'No,' Leila replied, 'I do not know whether he intended to sleep at his desert house last night or stay over here in Baghdad.'

'Please, oh please let me know as soon as you have some information,' she continued.

The Professor lived alone. He had two sons away studying in America and his wife had been an early victim of the Shi'a bombing campaign, some two years earlier.

The police investigation of his whereabouts proved to be totally unsuccessful and just a few days later, with no further contacts or evidence emerging, the file was put aside. They suspected that he had probably perished in the flames that had consumed his desert house. The Iraqi Police had many far more urgent and serious problems to confront with the daily carnage on the streets of this ancient city.

As for Leila, she was instructed by the Mossad to return to the Baghdad Museum and continue her Caliphate research at least until she received further orders.

**El Paso.**

Yossi slept soundly from the combined effects of the wine and the love making with Jilly. He awoke with a start to discover that it was nine o'clock in the morning. Turning over in the large double bed to confront his sleeping partner he found that she had already left the bed and presumably the suite. This she would have achieved quite easily without waking him. He realised ruefully that she could have left five minutes or five hours ago; such was the depth of his drink-induced sleep.

Yossi showered and dressed and was quite relieved to find that his body and brain were both functioning well despite the previous night's activities. He felt quite hungry and had resolved to go and find some breakfast when the door buzzer sounded. A glance at the screen told him it was his host the Rev. Bill Cooper. Yossi opened the door to discover his host with a thunderous expression on his face far different from his usual smiling and friendly disposition. Plainly the Rev. Bill was angry, very angry. He pushed past Yossi without saying a single word and strode across the room. He seated himself in a large armchair and from this vantage point he glared at Yossi. Yossi meanwhile closed the door to the suite and offered his host a cup of coffee.

'I am not here for coffee or chit-chat,' his host responded. 'I want you out of here this morning and you can tell your boss that my trip to Israel is off.'

'Why is that?' Yossi replied nervously. He had a pretty shrewd idea that he already knew the answer, but the question needed to be asked.

Rev. Bill stood up and pulled from his breast pocket what looked like two photographs.

'This is why I want nothing more to do with you or your country,' Bill replied, handing the pictures to a horrified Yossi.

'You Sir,' the Rev. Bill continued, 'are a fornicator and a seducer.'

Yossi glanced down at the photographs and realised that they showed him naked and in the most compromising of positions on the bed with the woman who called herself Jilly.

He could hardly deny an accusation of having had sex with Jilly; the evidence was there before him and no doubt there were many more such pictures. However to be called a seducer when from what he could remember of the previous night, she had virtually seduced him, seemed quite ridiculous.

'You took a respectable Christian lady and made her into a whore!' the Minister thundered.

'Pack your bags and get out,' the Rev. continued in his best rabble-rousing voice.

'Look,' Yossi began, 'there is some mistake here, can we at least talk about this?'

'There is nothing to say,' was the reply. 'I do not enter into dialogue with rapists and fornicators.'

Yossi was becoming quite desperate. He quickly realised that if he left without attempting some kind of resolution his country would suffer from the complete alienation of a loyal friend. Moreover, he would be out of a job and if the news ever reached the media as to why the Church of the Second Coming had suddenly withdrawn their support for Israel he would be lucky not to land up in jail. *In addition*, he speculated, *I should not have let myself be compromised by appearing on a stage with the Rev. Bill.*

'Please Sir,' Yossi tried again. 'Is there nothing I can do to make amends?'

Suddenly there was a change in the Minister's demeanour. He returned to his seat and turned to face Yossi with what could only be described as an evil little smile on his lips.

'Ok,' the Rev. ventured, 'sit down and let us see what can be done to repair the mess that your ungodly lust has landed you in.'

'I must tell you that what you did was unforgivable, however, it would be morally wrong to let your country and mine suffer for your lack of control.'

The Rev. Bill sat there, apparently deep in thought, for a few moments. When he spoke again it was as if all the anger he had displayed only a minute or two ago had vanished. Indeed he somehow gave the impression that he had never been angry or had any cause to be less than delighted with Yossi's visit.

'You know Yossi,' he began, smiling broadly. 'I so much appreciated your accompanying me to the meeting yesterday. I know you felt it might have been unwise to allow me to draw so much attention to you in public and in front of such a multitude of people. However, I cannot see how any harm can have been done and it was, in my opinion just another small boost for our cause.'

'And you know what our cause is, don't you Yossi?'

'Our cause,' he continued, without awaiting a reply, 'is a strong independent Israel as a homeland for the entire Jewish nation. And then we will really be able to welcome the return of our saviour.'

Yossi surveyed the minister in astonishment. One minute he was accused of being a fornicator and a rapist and the next minute only one step away from being a hero.

'I don't know what to say,' Yossi ventured.

'Say nothing my friend,' the Rev. Bill interrupted. 'We now have two little secrets between us. The first being your public appearance yesterday. I know you think that it may not go down too well with your boss. And the second is here on these photos. I will guard them, I promise you Yossi. I would really hate it for you to be embarrassed by your mistake last night. So Yossi, we have two little secrets, you and me. Let us hope they can always remain as such.'

By now Yossi was totally convinced that he had been deliberately compromised so that he would be well and truly in the power of this obviously evil man who called himself a minister of religion. He considered asking for the prints of the photographs, but he knew that the original digital images would already be locked away in some coded file of Bill's computer. All he could do, he quickly decided, was to appear grateful and try to get back to Israel as soon as possible.

Yossi tried to be as courteous and friendly as he could to this man who now had the ability to control him, but he knew the day would dawn when the Rev. Bill would call in the debt that he now owed him.

And so with a heavy heart Yossi returned to Israel to report to Ash on the highly successful outcome of his trip. If Ash only knew the truth!

**Amman.**

It had taken Craig hours to get to sleep. His brain was in turmoil and much as the ill treatment the terrorists had meted out to him had worried and scared him, he knew they were the enemy. He could hardly have expected any other behaviour from them. Now he was a prisoner, for no good reason that he could see, of his own people. How could they do this to him? He knew he had disobeyed orders in not sticking to the main desert road and that the consequence of that was the tragic death of his comrades. So, he agonised, arrest me, try me before a Courts Martial, but a least my family would know I am not dead.

He was awakened the following morning by a loud knock on the door and into the room came the Ambassador accompanied by a man he had never seen before. Although the man was dressed in casual clothes Craig's first thought was that he must be an officer from Basra, come to escort him back to base. Everything about the man seemed to indicate that he was of senior rank both in the army and probably socially as well. He was tall and had the blue eyes and blond hair that somehow seemed to mark him out as upper crust.

Craig knew instantly that when the man spoke he would have that public school drawl that even in this egalitarian age still marked him out as a member of the privileged class. Eton, Oxford and Sandhurst would have been his training ground and they had marked him as one of their own.

Craig jumped out of bed and stood to attention wearing only his pyjama trousers.

The Ambassador smiled and looked friendlier again.

'This is James Smyth. He has just arrived from London and is a member of the Security Service. I will leave you two together.'

James gave Craig a smile and said,

'Go and get some clothes on. I assume you would like some breakfast and so would I. We can talk as we eat. I am ravenous,' he confided.

Craig instantly liked this man despite their totally different backgrounds. Then he remembered that he had instantly liked the Ambassador. *These guys can turn on the charm like a tap,* he decided, *and turn it off again just as quickly.*

They breakfasted in the Ambassador's private quarters, but George Carmichael, the Ambassador, was nowhere to be seen. His companion's claim to be ravenous was confirmed by the manner in which he attacked the large breakfast. Craig ate with less enthusiasm, still deeply unhappy with yesterday's turn of events.

'Come on,' James said at one stage, 'have some more toast. I never met a sergeant with such a poor appetite.'

'I'm fine,' Craig replied, feeling far from fine.

'Right, my boy,' James eventually said, leaning back in the heavy wooden dining chair and patting his stomach. 'Let's talk.'

As Craig quickly discovered, that meant *let me talk!*

'Look, old boy,' he began. 'I know you have had a really rough time, but being in the army in Iraq can't exactly have been a picnic anyway.'

'I'm sorry, but it is absolutely vital that you remain officially dead. I know you must be desperate to tell your folks that you are alive and well, but right now you are of most use to the dear old UK as a non-person.'

'I just want to run through the short list of people who know you are alive and then I will tell you our plans.'

James listed the Professor, whom he explained to Craig was now missing, presumed dead himself, the Mossad people, Leila and Jack, and Prince Jamal of Jordan.

'We know that the Prince, for his own rather mysterious reasons, has not reported any of this affair to the King or the Jordanian government. If he was going to do this he should have done so right at the beginning. He is now compromised with his own people for withholding the information. Also, he has assured George Carmichael that what is written on these documents terrifies him and he would be the last person on earth to wish to divulge the contents of the scrolls. However, George feels he is rather overstating the case and may secretly have other ideas.'

'As for the Mossad operatives,' James continued, ' they both report directly to one senior man, Ash Giladi. He is the soul of discretion, a complete professional. There is only one weak link and that is the new Prime Minister of Israel. It was he who had involved Prince Jamal. However,' James continued, 'Israel would be one of the first casualties if the substance of the text in your scrolls became public. He knows that as well as anyone.'

At last Craig had his chance to interrupt.

'I found the scrolls and I am still the only person who knows exactly where they are. But what the hell is in them that so worries everyone?'

'Sergeant,' James responded flatly and not without menace, 'if I tell you the little, even I know, you must understand that any failure to co-operate and maintain absolute silence on this subject will result in your death becoming a reality.'

He made this statement as if it was the most natural thing in the world for a British Intelligence Agent to be threatening to kill one his countries loyal soldiers.

James obviously found it necessary to amplify what he had just said.

'The British Security Services do not usually threaten their own soldiers, but in the scheme of things your removal would become a national, no, an international necessity.'

Craig shuddered. He knew that men like James beneath the veneer of bonhomie were utterly ruthless.

Craig knew when he was beaten. He was a good British soldier and even without the threat to his existence he would never have dreamed of disobeying important orders. He had of course disobeyed a general order to stay on the main highways when out of town, but he could hardly have known what chain of events he had been setting in motion by this minor disobedience.

'Yes Sir,' Craig acknowledged, 'if you look at my record you will see that I am not in the habit of disobeying direct orders or betraying my country. It just grieves me to think about my family mourning me when all the time I am alive.

Suddenly James became more human again.

'Look here, old chap,' he said comfortingly, 'I do understand, but when you know the dangerous chain of events your discovery could ignite, you will understand why we need to keep you under wraps as a non-person.'

'Ok,' James continued, 'here goes. It seems that the contents of the two scrolls are identical. They constitute the same document but written in Hebrew for the Jews and Arabic for the Arabs. The only information we have been able to obtain is that these documents, written hundreds of years ago, were unknown until you found them. And they are enough to set the whole region alight, according to our Israeli sources.'

'As you know only too well,' James continued, 'there is now virtual civil war between the extremist Sunni Muslims and the fanatical Shi'a in Iraq. However, there are many decent sensible people on both sides of the religious divide who are trying to build bridges and unite the country.

If the content of your scrolls leaked out, from what we gather, there would be civil war throughout the Muslim world, even spilling over into the large communities in Britain, France and the USA.'

'You know and I know that the Israelis would never wish to publicise such a dangerous document. A major war between the Sunni and the Shi'a would drag in the entire Middle East on one side or the other. The Iranians may be keen to threaten Israel, but if they had the idea that the Jews were secretly in cahoots with the Sunni they would attack Israel and Jordan without a thought of the consequences. They would also foment insurrection in all countries with large Shi'a minorities and that would include Lebanon and Syria.'

'Then there is the problem of Saudi Arabia. They are Sunni, but for the last two hundred years they have been under the influence of the Wahabi sect of Sunni and they are just as fanatical as the Shi'a, but sworn enemies of each others brand of Islam.'

'Are you beginning to get the picture?' James enquired.

'Yes,' Craig answered, 'but I still do not see what in my document could cause such an outcry today. Surely,' Craig continued, 'if your information comes from Israel they will be passing it on to other countries'

'Look Craig,' James responded. 'I am certain that the Israelis would never want to publicise the document. They know only too well the sensitivities of the region. They know they would be lighting the fuse for an explosion that could destroy or seriously damage them.'

'We feel confident,' James continued, 'that the Israeli Security Services are far too sensible for that. But, if the knowledge of the very existence of this document was known to the Muslim nations and they knew the Israelis were aware of it, they would expect the Israelis to use it. And that is why **we must get hold of those scrolls before anyone else does.**'

### The Villa of Prince Jamal

That same morning, just a few miles away from the British Embassy, there was a telephone call for Prince Jamal.

When the servant answered the phone a well educated, but Iraqi accented Arabic speaker asked to speak to the Prince.

'Who shall I tell him is on the phone?' the servant quite reasonably enquired.

'Just tell him it is a friend of An-Nasir,' the man replied.

The servant was not satisfied. He needed a name to see whether the Prince would accept this phone call or not.

'Yes Sir,' the servant replied, 'but who shall I say is calling. Not your friend's name, but your name.'

The caller sounded mildly irritated. 'Just go and tell His Highness that I am a friend of An-Nasir, he will understand.'

'Very well Sir, but I doubt that the Prince will speak to you.'

The servant was quite wrong however.

'An-Nasir,' the Prince replied in astonishment when the servant reported the only details of the caller that he had. 'Did he say An-Nasir?'

'Yes your Highness,' the servant explained. 'I told him you would not speak with him unless he gave his own name, but he refused.'

'Put the call through at once,' the Prince responded sharply.

The Prince was seated in the library; an oak-panelled room with high shelves containing probably thousands of books in English, French and Arabic.

He lifted the handset.

'Hello this is Prince Jamal ibn Musa, is this who I think it is?' Then the Prince noticed that his servant was standing there obviously intent on ensuring he had done his best to protect his employer from unwanted phone calls.

'Just one minute,' the Prince said to the caller. Then turning to the servant he intoned,

'Thank you Hassan, that will be all.'

Recovering the handset he repeated the enquiry as to the identity of the caller.

He listened intently for a minute and then said,

'So where are you now?'

The reply obviously pleased him and he replaced the receiver and called for Hassan to return.

'Hassan, we have an honoured guest who will be arriving in about twenty minutes. Please ensure he gains entry without any of the usual interrogation and bring him straight to me. It is the same man who was just on the phone and he will tell you he is a friend of An-Nasir.'

The servant bowed and left the library.

It could only have been a matter of ten or fifteen minutes later when Hassan returned with the visitor.

'My dear Professor,' the Prince began, 'Ins'allah you are safe. I feared the worst when I heard about your house. What happened?'

'But first, forgive me! A cup of coffee, I am sure that will be welcome.'

Professor Sa'id leaned back in the armchair savouring the thick sweet Arab coffee.

'That was wonderful,' he exclaimed, 'now I feel like a human being again.'

The Professor leaned forward and gazed earnestly at his host.

'I have amazing things to tell you, dangerous things for us all, but nevertheless amazing. But first I have a question for you-How did you know about my house?'

'An Israeli agent called Jack told me,' the Prince explained.

'But how did he know-unless they were the ones who did the deed?'

'Listen Abdullah,' the Prince replied. 'I am sure they would not have done such a thing. You were no threat to them and they know of your close unofficial ties with Professor Eliezer Meiri of the Hebrew University.'

'Then how did they know so quickly?'

'I think their agent Sheherezade must have reported,' the Prince explained.

'And who is Sheherazade?' the Professor retorted showing a slight amount of irritation with the Prince's obviously superior knowledge of the Israeli Security Service.

'She is one of their agents in Iraq,' the Prince replied, 'and she is absolutely charming. She was here only yesterday when we tried to interrogate the English Sergeant. What a stubborn man!' he concluded.

'Did you say the British Sergeant?' The Professor replied becoming more astonished by the second.

'What was this Sergeant's name?'

The Prince was almost enjoying the situation.

'Oh Craig something?' he replied.

'Craig Blackburn, Sergeant Craig Blackburn, and with respect how on earth did Craig Blackburn get here?' the Professor quizzed the Prince.

'Oh, the Israelis and I think the Americans helped,' he replied.

The Prince was becoming a little impatient with his old friend. The Professor had arrived and announced that he had important information, but all he seemed to be doing was asking questions.

On reflection the Professor realised that he owed the Prince an explanation.

'Just two days ago Craig Blackburn was a guest in my house and now he turns up in Jordan with a bunch of Israelis. Now maybe you will understand my surprise.'

The Professor did not want to use the term 'prisoner.' Guest sounded so much better.

'In your house?' the Prince repeated a little intrigued. The Israelis had not told him where the British Sergeant had been held.

It was time to discover exactly what each of these men knew by an open and frank exchange of information.

'I think I already know quite a lot about what you are going to tell me. You see I have seen the photos of the scrolls.'

'Our problem,' the Prince continued, 'is that they are incredibly dangerous and we need to find the originals. I am sure the British will now know where they are, but they don't seem to want to tell anyone.'

'Well there is one small piece of good news in all this. The Israelis have no more idea where the scrolls are than we do. Their agent in Iraq, Sheherezade, was doing her level best to persuade the British soldier to tell her, but he did not succumb even to her very considerable charms.'

'With respect, your Highness,' the Professor replied, 'can we now please know a little more about this Sheherezade?'

'Certainly, my friend,' the Prince answered. 'She is very beautiful, about thirty years old and she speaks perfect Arabic with an Iraqi accent.'

'Obviously Sheherezade is not her real name,' the Professor probed.

'No,' the Prince replied enjoying the opportunity to be able once again to lecture to a Professor of Abdullah's reputation. 'I heard the agent known as Jack call her Leila.'

The Professor gasped. 'Did you say Leila?'

'Yes,' replied the Prince.

Now it was the Prince's turn to be shocked.

'She is my assistant,' the Professor mumbled as the sheer enormity of the situation dawned on him.

'No wonder you have been talking about the Israelis ever since I arrived,' the Professor continued.

'So they know all about An-Nasir's Declaration,' the Professor commented, still absolutely shattered to learn that his valued assistant was an Israeli spy.

'So the Israelis know about the Declaration as you call it!' The Prince repeated.

'Yes and the only reason I know is because the new Israeli Prime Minister sent me a coded message about it. He wanted us to work together in finding the scrolls.'

'Then they will use this Declaration, as you call it, to strengthen their claim to Palestine,' the Professor commented. 'They will say that an Arab Prince, An-Nasir, promised them the land long before the British Balfour Declaration.'

'No they won't,' the Prince replied. 'If they were going to go public with the document they would not have involved me. I have had three long telephone conversations with their PM Yigal Shomroni since yesterday. They will never use the text as they believe that the Shi'a would immediately condemn all Sunni Muslims and use this as a pretext to attack us and overthrow our governments. And we in Jordan would be the first to go, or so they think.' the Prince finished.

'And they feel that would be disaster for us and a very serious problem for Israel,' he continued. 'I am sure you know that although we are loyal Arabs we have managed to get on pretty well with the Israelis for some time now. For our government to be replaced by a fanatical Shi'a regime would be as big a disaster for them as it would be for us.'

From the minute that Professor Sa'id had read the Arabic text, downloaded from Craig's phone he had realised all this. His house had been destroyed and he had hoped that his personal computer and Craig's phone, left in the house, would also have gone up in flames. He had no idea what had happened to Craig or to Leila, his assistant, until the Prince confided that they had been in Amman. And now he had discovered that she was an Israeli spy. However, the men who had originally kidnapped Craig had also read the Declaration. He had no idea if they had survived the fire or not, and for all he knew, they might have started it. He had decided to leave Iraq quietly and visit his old friend Prince Jamal to ask his advice as to what action could be taken to suppress the knowledge of the existence of the scrolls. He had used the name An-Nasir because he knew that the Prince would realise that only his old college friend Professor Sa'id would use that name. If people in Iraq thought he had perished in the fire, so be it. Like Craig he had become, at least for the time being, a non-person.

'There is only one thing for it,' the Prince continued, **'we must get hold of those scrolls before anyone else does.'**

**Somewhere in the Negev Desert.**

Jack had returned to report to Ash that all their endeavours to discover the location of the scrolls had been totally unsuccessful. The British Sergeant Craig Blackburn had behaved exactly as Jack would have behaved himself, had their roles been reversed. By now the British Foreign Office would undoubtedly know from the Ambassador where Craig had found the documents and Jack was sure they would not be in any hurry to tell anyone else.

Leila was now in Baghdad, but without Professor Sa'id she was unable to help. And what had happened to Professor Sa'id? His house had been burned to the ground and there was a strong possibility that he had perished in the flames. Was this also the fate of the four terrorists who had kidnapped Craig Blackburn? Jack had told the Jordanian Prince that his men had disposed of them, but the truth was that they were nowhere to be found when the Israelis entered and subsequently left with Sheherezade and Craig. That had been a mistake, Jack decided, but probably a harmless one as he was certain that the Prince had not believed him and desperately needed to hear that the four men were really out of the equation.

Ash was deep in thought. Jack sat opposite him waiting for further instructions. He had an uncomfortable idea of what those instructions would be.

Eventually Ash spoke.

'Jack, we are going to fix you up with a new identity and a British passport to match. Then we are going to send you back to Iraq as a visiting British businessman. This time,' he continued, 'you will probably be away for quite a while.'

Jack had been right. This was exactly the course of action he had anticipated. The dangers for all foreign visitors to Iraq were still very great and British and American businessmen were top of the hit list for terrorist groups. There was only one thing worse than being in Iraq as a Briton and that was to be captured there as an Israeli. Jack had the misfortune of being both.

'You will receive full instructions later on today, but in the meantime I will arrange for the passport to be prepared.'

Jack nodded. He was a brave man and had been abroad on many dangerous assignments, but he felt quite sick at the prospect of what lay before him. However, he had joined the Mossad to help his country in whatever manner he was called upon and with an involuntary sigh he excused himself from Ash's office to await final instructions.

Ash knew that even if it all went as well as it possibly could, Jack would probably be out of Israel for some weeks. As a consequence his desk job, acting as liaison to Sheherazade would have to be temporarily allocated to someone else.

Half an hour after Jack had unhappily departed from Ash's office, Yossi was summoned into the sanctum. Since his return from the disastrous visit to Rev. Bill Cooper, Yossi had behaved as the loyal, conscientious operative he really was. Ash had no reason to doubt him and to enable him to take over the Southern Iraq desk Yossi was thoroughly briefed regarding the two scrolls. Ash spelled out, in no uncertain terms, the Armageddon that could ensue if the world's media obtained this information. Yossi fully understood and was determined to undertake his new, if temporary, appointment with total discretion.

Within twenty four hours Jack Baker of the Mossad, born in Prestwich, a suburb of Manchester with a large Jewish population, had been transformed into John Bradshaw a building engineer from Worsley - a predominately non-Jewish area of the same city. Both areas were fairly affluent and both would produce men with a similar accent, education and background.

This time there would be no requests for co-operation from the Jordanians or the Americans. Jack was flown across to Cyprus and from there he was booked on to a direct flight to Baghdad. His first task on arrival was to check in at the Al Mansour Hotel. Then he had to wait for Sheherazade to contact him. Finally, after drinking innumerable cups of coffee, there was a gentle knock on his door. Having checked that it was indeed Sheherazade or Leila, as he preferred to call her when they were together, he opened the door and ushered her into his suite.

The only way they could discover the location of the scrolls was from the British and they would be in no hurry to co-operate. There could be no doubt that the SIS (British Intelligence) would try to recover the documents before anyone else discovered their whereabouts. They were equally sure that the Jordanians would also be following the same agenda.

'Tomorrow, Mr Bradshaw,' Leila said, 'Ash wants you to go to the British Embassy and to register as a visiting British businessman. And while you are there you must try and discover if anything unusual is afoot. **We must get hold of those scrolls before anyone else does**.'

### Jerusalem
### An Unwelcome Visitor.

To most Israelis the news of the arrival of one of their most loyal Christian friends from the USA was greeted very positively. The new Prime Minister Yigal Shomroni called personally at the King David Hotel in Jerusalem to welcome the Rev. Bill Cooper. The Jerusalem Post ran an in-depth article about the visitor and his unfailing financial and political support for the Jewish State. The Rev. Bill was treated almost like the head of a friendly state and he held court in the majestic old hotel to a succession of visiting Churchmen, Rabbis and politicians. The only absentees from this parade of the great and the good of Israel were the senior Muslim clerics. Throughout the Rev. Bill's career as a preacher he had made it patently clear that he regarded Islam as an aberration from the true path to God and its adherents he treated with contempt. So vehement was his condemnation, particularly after the 9/11 bombing of the World Trade Centre in New York, that both Christians and Jews found this aspect of his Ministry to be something of an embarrassment. However, he was a great

Christian preacher and had brought many thousands back in to the fold. For this reason, most of the other Protestant sects treated him with respect while they tried to distance themselves from his more aggressive anti-Islamic statements. To the Orthodox and Roman churches he was an enigma. He constantly alluded to their brands of Christianity as being misguided, but his political influence was so vast that they tolerated him and his occasional outbursts against them.

The Israelis feted him as a great friend, but they were more than aware of his true agenda. Jews throughout the world knew that his friendship and political clout was there because he preached that with the return of all the world's Jews to Israel, there would be a Second Coming and that would entail the conversion of the entire world, including the Jews, to his brand of Christianity. However, in the meantime they enthusiastically welcomed their great supporter and tried to capitalise on the positive aspects of his friendship.

The Rev. Bill had been greeted at the airport by a large number of politicians, senior military men and of course religious leaders. He had been whisked away, as quickly as possible by Security Men including members of the Mossad. Rev. Bill was disappointed however, that the Mossad man he most needed to see in the welcoming party, Yossi, was nowhere to be seen.

The first two days of his visit were very busy, but not so busy that he was able to ignore the absence of any contact from Yossi. It was not because the Minister had any special liking for the younger Mossad man, but Rev. Bill had made it a matter of priority to compromise Yossi on his recent visit to the USA so that he could use him for his own benefit when the situation required it. He had fully expected Yossi to be at the airport. Had Ash not appointed Yossi to be his liaison and to ensure the trip passed off without a hitch? So where on earth was he?

On the third day he decided to enquire as to what had happened to Yossi from one of the other Mossad men.

'Oh he has been assigned to other special duties,' his informant explained. 'Something very hush-hush, that is all I know and in any case whatever he is working on is high security so they would not tell me. That is the way we work. Information only on a need to know basis.'

The Rev. Bill was intrigued and a little insulted. Surely his visit was as important as anything else. After consideration he decided it was only natural that he should wish to see the officer who had sorted out the security for his entire trip. He had spoken to Ash on the telephone during the visit and he resolved to call him again and ask why Yossi had not been assigned to him.

'Something came up and I needed to put one of my best men on to it,' Ash explained a little testily. Why on earth did he have to explain the disposition of his own men to this American Preacher?

'But I would have liked to have seen him to say thank you,' Rev. Bill explained. 'Yossi did all the planning and now I cannot even tell him how pleased I am with his work.'

'Leave it with me,' Ash replied wearily. He had strict instructions to keep the Minister happy and if that meant borrowing Yossi from the Iraq desk for a couple of hours it would have to be done.

The Rev. Bill had just finished dressing for his scheduled dinner with the leader of the Israel Labour Party when there was a knock at the door. His security man checked who was there and then ushered the visitor in to the room. It was Yossi.

Yossi was far from pleased to have been taken off a top-secret assignment to play nursemaid to this man who had already caused him so much trouble and heartache on the previous occasion on which they had met. He was a worried man. He knew what was at stake in Iraq with the search for the two scrolls. He also knew that the Rev. Bill was far from the God-fearing preacher that he made himself out to be. The man was dangerous, very dangerous and he had the knowledge to make life very difficult indeed for Yossi.

However, Yossi knew how to cover-up his real feelings towards the Minister.

'Hello Bill,' he began with as much warmth as he could muster. 'It is good to see you here in Israel. I believe you asked my boss Ash if I could see you.'

'Sure Yossi,' the Rev. Bill replied. 'We got on so well stateside that I expected you would be with me all the way on this trip.'

'That was the intention,' the Mossad man replied, 'but I was transferred to other duties.'

'Wow,' the Minster replied, 'does that mean promotion? See what happens when you have the Church of the Second Coming on your side.'

'Look Yossi,' Bill continued, 'I had hoped we would have lots of time to talk, but I guess you will soon have to get back to your new assignment. I would love to see inside Mossad HQ while I am here. Can you fix that for me?'

'Sorry Bill,' Yossi replied. 'That is totally impossible. Even Israeli government ministers are often denied access to our top-secret facilities.'

'Yossi,' the Minister replied threateningly, 'if you are refusing me, I think I need to remind you that with what I know about you and your behaviour in America you could easily be out of the Mossad HQ yourself and permanently.'

This was just what Yossi had been dreading. It was payback time. However, what was being asked of him was totally beyond his control.

'Look Bill,' Yossi explained, 'I have no authority to admit anyone, and I mean anyone to our HQ. Even Ash the head of my section could not do what you are asking. There are passes to obtain, checkouts to pass and there is just no way. Believe me, I would help if I could, but it is impossible.' he finished lamely.

The Minister considered the Mossad man's response and seemed to accept it.

'Ok,' he said finally, 'lets have a drink and I will let you get back to work.'

**Baghdad**
**Ibrahim.**

John Bradshaw otherwise known as Jack Baker arrived at 11am to keep his appointment at the British Embassy. First, he was ushered into the office of an Iraqi National called Hamid Ashraf who was a senior employee of the Embassy and whose job it was to give all possible assistance to visiting foreign businessmen. The man known as John Bradshaw quickly explained that he was in Iraq to advise on the construction of a shopping mall and market place in the South of the country. This project was public knowledge and the Israelis quickly decided that it gave reason enough to justify the necessity to call in a British Building Engineer. So this became Jack's cover.

Jack explained that he had just arrived and simply wished to register the fact with the Embassy. He told Hamid that he would certainly need assistance in such matters as personal security and having made his presence known, he left the office of the helpful official.

The Embassy was a hive of activity and Jack's real purpose in visiting the building was to try and gain some information about what steps the British were taking to locate the scrolls. His first task was to locate an Embassy official by the name of Graham Jackson. His public remit was Trade, but the Senior Embassy staff and the Israeli Security Service knew that this was just a cover and that he was in fact one of the most senior SIS men in Iraq. What the Embassy staff did not know was that he was also a loyal friend of Israel and in return for generous payments, had often provided valuable information to the Mossad. As far as Graham was concerned Israel, the UK and the USA were all engaged as allies in the same fight to see real democracy, peace and freedom permanently installed in the Middle East and to win the war against terror. He saw no harm in accepting some major donations to his Swiss bank account if they were in such a good cause.

When Jack had telephoned for an appointment, Jackson's PA had tried to deflect him to a more genuine Trade official.

'Look,' Jack had explained, 'Roger Anderson at the Foreign Office said I must see Mr Jackson personally.'

So a few minutes after leaving Hamid's office, Jack was sitting opposite Graham chatting merrily about Jack's forthcoming trip to the South, the shopping mall and various other associated matters.

After an hour or so Graham suggested that they leave the Embassy to go and have a light lunch. Graham had long ago selected the restaurant as a place where he and his associates would be safe from eavesdroppers, either conventional or electronic. Whenever he needed a confidential chat this was where he went.

The Al-Rashid Restaurant was always quiet at lunchtime and really came into its own in the evening when it was patronised by a wide clientele comprising diplomatic personnel and the more prominent media people. When Jack and Graham arrived there were only three other tables occupied.

Jack casually glanced around the large room as soon as they were seated. His only other visit to Iraq had been just a few days earlier to rescue the British sergeant. He was confident that no one would know him in Baghdad, but nevertheless Mossad training had taught him to leave nothing to chance. Being satisfied that there were no familiar faces the two men got down to the serious business of ordering their meal. They decided on a light lunch consisting of a delicious salad inserted inside the huge pita-bread for which the country was famous. They ate in silence only ceasing when their plates were empty. Then they sat back and sipped small cups of sweet Arabic coffee. Finally Jack spoke.

'I think you will have guessed why I am in Baghdad and what I wanted to see you about,' he suggested.

'Come on Jack,' Graham replied, 'you know I don't go in for guessing games. If you want me to be upfront with you, you must be upfront with me.'

'Ok,' Jack responded, carefully choosing his words. 'I am here regarding two ancient scrolls, a British Sergeant called Craig Blackburn and an Iraqi Professor.'

'And would this Iraqi Professor happen to have disappeared?' The SIS man answered, with a smile.

'Yes and what do you know about his house in the South?' the Mossad man replied.

'Ok,' Graham answered a little wearily. 'It was razed to the ground just a couple of nights ago.'

'As for the scrolls, we know little of what they contain, but we sure as hell know that whatever it is, it is upsetting everybody. You guys, the Jordanians and there appears to be a small pocket of Iraqi Sunni insurgents, are all very anxious to find them.'

'As for us,' the SIS man continued, 'we know from our Sergeant Blackburn what a devastating effect they have on everyone who reads them. We also know where they are, but we do not know properly what they contain. Here is the deal,' he proposed, 'I am prepared to give you that information if you explain in detail what is so special about them.'

Their table was at the rear of the restaurant and close to the door leading to the kitchens. Jack decided to provide his information. He knew that Graham would hardly go back on the deal particularly when he could add to his Swiss bank nest egg by doing so.

'Ok, here goes,' Jack began. 'There was a Caliph here about a thousand years ago called An-Nasir...' That was as far as he got when they heard the sound of someone entering the restaurant. They both looked over to see the outline of two men standing in the now open doorway. It took only another second to recognise that they were both pointing handguns in the direction of their table.

'Quick get down under the table,' Graham yelled, but a bullet to the chest cut off his words as he slumped forward. Jack in the meantime had quickly slid under the table and was surprised to hear the chatter of automatic fire coming, just seconds later, from one of the other tables in the restaurant. Peering out nervously he could see along the passage separating the rows of tables, that there now appeared to be two bodies lying in the doorway. Then he saw that his companion was still sitting and he tapped him on the leg. This brought no response. Then Jack saw that someone was approaching the table. He already had his own handgun at the ready, but held his fire suspecting that Graham, apparently still sitting at the table would have seen and disposed of the attacker if such he was.

'Oh my God,' a strange voice intoned in American accented English. 'Come out buddy, they certainly won't fire again.'

Jack stood up to see the stranger, a tall black man in a smart business suit, tapping Graham on the shoulder. This brought no response and between them they lifted his head and shoulders to see a bloody gaping hole in the SIS man's chest. Meanwhile the waiter had called an ambulance and the Iraqi police, who both arrived with amazing rapidity. Graham was dead, very dead and Jack shuddered when he considered how near he had been to the same fate. The two gunmen were also dead, killed by a rain of fire from the black American's weapon.

It took two hours for the Iraqi police to take statements from Jack and the American, who introduced himself as Tom Robinson. The waiter had been in the kitchen when all this occurred and could add little to the story. The small number of other diners had left before the shooting and only this solitary American had remained. How thankful Jack was that Tom Robinson had taken a leisurely lunch that day. He had saved Jack's life.

British Embassy officials had been called and they also interviewed the waiter, Tom Robinson and the man introduced to them as John Bradshaw, building engineer. They were a little suspicious as to why a top SIS man would be lunching with a civilian building engineer, but although very shaken, Jack was able to satisfy all their questions. Eventually, with the three bodies removed for further forensic examination, Jack and Tom were allowed to leave the now darkened restaurant.

As Jack bent down to retrieve his briefcase on the floor by the table, he noticed that on the tablecloth there appeared to be something written in the blood of poor Graham. Peering at it, he could just make out what appeared to be the name 'Ibrahim.' He then realised that Graham, in his dying seconds, had managed to write the word. *What was its significance*, he pondered, but no inspiration presented itself. *Ibrahim is a common enough name throughout the Arab world*, he decided. *Was this the name of one of the assassins?* He wondered.

In the meantime Tom had retrieved his own briefcase from his table and his small automatic weapon had disappeared into one of the large pockets of the loose leather jacket he wore, almost in defiance of the heat. Outside the restaurant, now guarded as a crime scene by an Iraqi policeman, Jack had requested Tom's card, but when the latter appeared reluctant, Jack did not persevere. He had no wish to supply his own contact information and regretted making the request as soon as he had uttered the words. They made their farewells and Jack returned to the hotel to await a call from Leila.

**Baghdad.**
**The British Embassy**
While Jack was experiencing the traumatic events at the Al-Rashid Restaurant, two visitors were about to arrive at the British Embassy less than half a mile away. One of the visitors was well known to the security establishment there. He was James Smyth, a senior SIS officer from London. His companion was a tall dark-haired young man with a thick moustache and spectacles.

The two men arrived just as the news broke of the assassination of Graham Jackson at the Al-Rashid Restaurant. James was a long time friend and colleague of Graham and the shock of receiving this information, just as he arrived at the Embassy, momentarily penetrated his usual sang-froid. James quickly recovered and realised that he was now the senior intelligence officer present in Baghdad and after a half- hour conference with the Ambassador, he set about investigating the tragic incident. As for his travelling companion, he was left to settle into their quarters at the Embassy until James could once again concentrate on the project that had originally brought them to this war-torn city.

James' first task was to interview all the security personnel who had worked with Graham. None of them were able to add to the well-known fact that in Iraq generally and in Baghdad in particular, it had now been open season for some time on all foreigners and particularly British and

American foreigners. This was not a comfortable city in which to work. If insurgents were not bombing each other and innocent Iraqis trying to go about their business, they were shooting and kidnapping visitors. This was a fact that newsreels all over the world reported daily. However, the shooting of a senior British Diplomat, even if he was secretly a member of SIS, was unusual to put it mildly.

Next James contacted the local police and arranged for an Inspector to visit him at the Embassy. Inspector Yacoub arrived promptly and was immediately escorted to James' office.

The pair discussed the assassination in some detail and the policeman was more than helpful with the information he supplied. He confided that the names of the two dead insurgents were Ali and Fuad and that they were brothers currently domiciled in the Basra area, where they were wanted by both the Iraqi police and the British administration. Their names had been linked to the torching of the desert home of Professor Sa'id, but only because they had been seen repeatedly in the vicinity before the fire.

At the mention of Professor Sa'id, James had began to suspect that somehow there must be a connection between the reason for his visit, the ancient scrolls, and the assassination of poor Graham. The men's names, of course, meant nothing to James, but there was other information that was even more intriguing. James already knew from the Embassy staff that Graham had gone out to lunch with a visiting British Building Engineer by the name of John Bradshaw and that this man had registered on arrival at the Embassy earlier that day. He resolved to check out Mr Bradshaw as soon as possible. A building engineer seemed to be an unlikely companion for an SIS operative. Then there was the matter of the American who had shot the two terrorists. The police had interviewed him and ascertained that his name was Tom Robinson. He was supposedly a civilian in the employ of the US army. That should be easy to check providing the information he had given to the police was correct.

As soon as Inspector Yacoub had departed, James went in search of the man with whom he had arrived at the Embassy. He found that having been allocated a room, his companion had settled down to watch TV and feed his addiction for Arab coffee. He had also, much to James' horror, removed his spectacles and although his hair was dyed black, he was fairly easily recognisable as Sergeant Craig Blackburn.

'You must keep those glasses on at all times.' James instructed. 'You are on British territory here and there is always the chance that some visiting member of the military from Basra, could recognise you. That would seriously compromise our security when we travel down to where you say these scrolls are to be found.'

'Craig,' the SIS man continued, 'you did say that the man who had you under virtual house arrest was Professor Sa'id?'

'Yes,' Craig responded. 'Nice bloke really! A gentleman and he did save me from almost certain death at the hands of the four terrorists I told you about.'

'Craig,' James continued, 'do you know the names of the four terrorists who kept you as their prisoner when you were first kidnapped?'

'Yes Sir,' Craig replied. 'Let me think. They were Mahmoud and Ali and Usama. I won't forget that one, it sounds like Osama bin Laden. Now what was the name of the fourth one?'

'No, I can't remember, sorry! I am sure it will come back to me.'

'Was it Fuad?' James enquired.

'Yes, that was it, Fuad! I think he might have been Ali's brother. They looked alike and appeared closer than the other two.'

'Well I have news for you. Both Ali and Fuad are dead,' he explained bitterly, ' but only after they managed to murder a fine old friend of mine.'

Craig had lost a number of his old friends in Iraq. Some in action and others in terrorist outrages and he still had to live with the memory of what had happened to his three companions when he went off to investigate the Cave of Ibrahim. He could see that behind the façade of his 'stiff upper lip' companion, James was deeply saddened.

However, the SIS man quickly reverted to his brusque public school manner and informed Craig that he must remain in his room at the Embassy and on no account venture down the stairs to the main lobby. His meals were to be brought to him by Iraqi kitchen staff.

'Just take advantage of the opportunity to relax,' James instructed. 'Once we go out into the desert to find this cave of yours, there will be no chance of resting.'

The following morning James telephoned the American head quarters in Baghdad and arranged to see one of the senior intelligence officers.

'Look old chap,' he explained, 'one of your civilian staff shot dead two terrorists in a restaurant yesterday. Sadly they had already managed to murder my old friend Graham Jackson.'

'Yes,' Agent Cooper replied, 'we heard all about that from the Iraqi police and we are undertaking our own investigation. I knew Graham pretty well.' He continued. 'Look James, can I level with you?'

'Of course,' James answered, 'that is exactly why I am here.'

'There are a number of very strange aspects to this case. Not least is the fact that we have two unidentifiable guys in the frame.'

'You don't mean the terrorists do you?' James replied smiling grimly.

'No, old buddy, I do not mean the terrorists, they were only too easy to identify.'

'You may be able to help to ID one of the mystery guys,' the American continued. 'Who the hell is John Bradshaw? We checked with your people yesterday afternoon. They told us he was a Building Engineer newly arrived in Baghdad. He was supposed to be involved in a development in your territory in the South, but he was not expected and no one had heard of him down there. And what is more, our agents in London tell us that no one there has any record of him.'

'Sorry, I can't help you,' James replied. 'I did all the same checks as you and drew a blank. I was very curious as to why Graham Jackson would be lunching with a Building Engineer.'

'Anyway, maybe your man Tom Robinson could help,' James suggested. 'He may have caught snatches of conversation from the other two guys' table?'

Now it was the American's turn to apologise.

'We do not employ a Tom Robinson. The only Tom Robinson who ever worked here was a little white clerk who was here in the early days of Sadam Hussein.'

'The man we are after is a tall good-looking black man and at the moment we have no trace of him or how he got into the country.'

'Well my friend,' James said, rising to leave, 'we both have a lot of work to do.'

## Hotel Al –Mansour.

When Jack arrived back at the hotel he immediately tried to contact Leila. He realised that the sooner he was away from Baghdad and certainly from the areas frequented by British and American personnel, the better.

Fortunately Leila was in the building and within minutes was at his door.

Jack quickly told her what had transpired at the hotel.

'With their man shot dead, the British are going to want to contact me. I have already given a statement to the Iraqi police and it can't be long before someone in SIS starts to wonder why a Senior Intelligence Officer was lunching with a Building Engineer.'

'You are right,' Leila replied. 'Did you tell the Iraqi police where you were staying?'

'Of course not,' Jack answered, a little hurt that she would even consider that he would give out the correct contact information.

'I said I was at the Palestine International Hotel. Rather apt don't you think? But I bet by now the Police are already there with the British searching for me.'

'Ok,' said Leila, thinking on her feet, 'you must get out of here at once. Leave your personal belongings in the room and just walk out of the lobby as if you are on your way to a meeting.'

'Just bring the British passport and some cash.' She instructed.

'Just one more thing! You registered at the British Embassy. Where did you tell them you were staying?'

'The Ishtar,' Jack replied grinning despite himself.

'Right Jack,' Leila told him, 'This address is not so far from here, but you must not take a taxi until you are at least 500 metres away from the hotel. Then only take it to Suleiman Street. From there you can walk. It is as safe as anywhere can be in this city. You are still inside the Green Zone, but be careful.'

She handed him a set of keys and sent him on his way to her apartment. Then she set about checking his few belongings for any telltale signs that would confirm who he really was. She had no doubt that the room would soon be searched by the Iraqi police and possibly by the British security people. There must be no way of connecting John Bradshaw of Manchester with a

Mossad agent called Jack. Everything was clean so she quietly let herself out of the room and strolled nonchalantly out of the lobby on to the street.

As she left she saw that an Iraqi police car had just drawn up outside the hotel. Two senior policemen jumped out. A very British-looking man accompanied them, as they entered the hotel. She sighed with relief when she realised how near to disaster they had been.

Leila was very sorry that Graham had been killed. She had found him to be something of an enigma. He had been utterly dedicated to the fight against world terror. He loved his country and the democratic way of life that the USA, the UK and Israel exemplified. He was a man with a considerable degree of personal charm and Leila considered him to be a loyal friend. How he had reconciled all this with his willingness to go the extra mile for his friends, in return for cash inducements, she found difficult to fathom. *Anyway,* she pondered, *the poor guy is dead. Whatever money he had stashed away can't help him now.*

### An Honoured Guest.

Just a few minutes after Jack and Leila had left the hotel, a large car arrived with escorts of outriders from the Iraqi police and American military. The hotel manager was there to greet the honoured guest and to escort him to his suite. It was the first time a senior member of the Jordanian royal family had visited Iraq for many a long year.

'Prince Jamal ibn Musa,' the hotel manager exclaimed obsequiously, 'this is a great honour.'

Two middle-aged male servants accompanied the Prince. One of the servants sported a thick beard and was wearing the traditional Keffiyeh loose in the manner of the Druze so that most of his face was hidden. The other servant, once he had put away the Prince's clothing and private possessions in his suite, bowed and left for his own quarters leaving just the full bearded man with the Prince.

As soon as they were alone, the bearded servant pulled off his Keffiyeh and then in a manner that would have amazed any onlookers, of whom fortunately there were none, removed what proved to be a very well constructed false beard.

'Am I glad to get rid of that,' the learned Professor Sa'id exclaimed.

'Please sit down,' the Prince replied, 'we have many plans to make.'

### Meanwhile - Somewhere in the Negev

Standing in for Jack had soon made Yossi realise the tremendous extra pressure that the discovery of the Scrolls was placing on the Iraq department of the Mossad. They were all working long shifts and although news had been sparse, the report of the assassination of Graham Jackson, the SIS man, had only increased Ash's concern and determination to find the scrolls. There had to be a connection. They knew that the terrorists who had murdered the British Intelligence officer must somehow be involved. In all likelihood it was Jack, the Mossad case officer who they were after.

However they were unaware that the two gunmen were part of the foursome who had imprisoned Craig, the British Sergeant.

In the meantime the Rev. Bill Cooper was still domiciled at the King David Hotel in Jerusalem from where he made pilgrimages to numerous Christian sites throughout the country. He was received like a Head of State and the organisation he controlled was virtually like a State within a State not only within the USA, but also in many other parts of the globe. Because of his huge following and charismatic character he was treated with circumspection wherever he went. In addition, because of his vehement condemnation of Islam and to a lesser extent of the Roman Church, he had many enemies. As a result he had gradually built up his own security organisation. From a small start with just one bodyguard he now had some twenty men on his payroll whose task it was not only to guard him and his immediate entourage, but also to act as his eyes and ears in many of the world's trouble spots. These men did not physically accompany him on his trips. Their job was to gather useful information, usually political, but by one means or another to be used to spread the Church's word and influence. They were known as the Secret Ambassadors of the Church of the Second Coming.

It was one of the most senior of these security men who sent him a coded message while the minister was in Israel. The message was marked urgent and stated as follows:

*Baghdad. 16th June 2006. Firstly and briefly my talks with the Christian Protestant leader Emile Hajjar went well. I will report fully on this on my return. However, there is something else going on here that you should know about. A Senior British SIS officer was murdered in my presence at the Al-Rashid Restaurant. He was there with another Englishman who looked as if he might have been Jewish. I shot the two terrorists myself otherwise the Jew, if such he was, and I would probably have also been killed. However, their conversation before the shooting was very interesting. As you know I always carry bugs. This may often be a waste of time but it sure paid off today!*

*I can tell you that the Jewish-looking Englishman was called Jack and they started to exchange information on some very strange subject.*

*This Jack said he was there regarding two ancient scrolls, a British Sergeant called Craig Blackburn and an Iraqi Professor. It appears that the Iraqi Professor had disappeared and even more curious, in what appeared to be a separate incident, his house had been burned down.*

*They both knew about the scrolls, whatever they were, but the SIS man said he did not have full details of what they contained. Then they discussed the anxiety of the Jordanians and a small pocket of Iraqi Sunni insurgents to locate them.*

*They both knew the name of the British Sergeant and he had apparently told somebody what a devastating effect these scrolls had on everyone who read them. The other Englishman, the SIS one, said the Brits knew where these scrolls were. He then offered to tell the guy called Jack the location if Jack in turn wised him up about the full content. A neat exchange of information!*

*Jack agreed and then started to talk about a Caliph, about a thousand years ago called An-Nasir... That was as far as he got when the terrorists entered the restaurant, opened fire and shot the SIS guy.*

*I am sure this is important. It may be useful for us politically and it might be a way of further discrediting Islam from one of their own documents. Anything is possible.*

*I was due to leave Baghdad tomorrow for Kuwait. Shall I hang on and try to get more information on all this?*

*There is just one problem. The police questioned me after the incident and I told them I was an employee of the American military. I used to be, but I ain't now, as well you know. Also the guy called Jack, the Jewish looking one, spoke to me outside the restaurant when the police let us go. He wanted my contact details. I politely refused to give them to him. What worries me is that I might be recognised either by him or the police. I will try to change my appearance, but it is a risk.*

The Rev. Bill read and re-read the communication. This certainly did look interesting. *I only wish,* he decided, *that all my men were as bright as Henry Roberts.* There was just one thing that Henry appeared not to have realised. If the Jewish looking Englishman had information that the SIS man did not have, they must be working for different organisations. *I am sure we will find out that the one called Jack, the Jewish looking one, is an Israeli of English origin. I bet he is a Mossad man and if I am right, my friend, Yossi, will know all about him.*

A phone call to Yossi's direct line, originally supplied by no lesser person than Ash before Yossi's American trip, was answered by voice mail.

'Yossi,' the Rev. Bill instructed. 'Call me as soon as you can. There is something I need to check with you.'

That sounded innocuous enough, he decided. If someone else picked up the message, he could always say he wanted to know about some aspect of his forthcoming trip to Ramallah to meet the Palestinian President. He was sincerely worried about this foray into 'enemy territory', but he had promised Church leaders in the USA that he would try to intercede on behalf of the shrinking number of unhappy Palestinian Christians inside the Authority area.

Then the Rev. Bill sent off a coded reply to Henry Roberts, his man in Baghdad.

*You were one hundred percent right to report this to me. Please do everything you can to get more details of what the Scrolls contain and where they are. Disguise yourself as necessary, but do not leave Iraq. **It sounds as if we need to get hold of these scrolls before anyone else does.***

### Leila's Apartment

The evening after the shooting, Jack and Leila discussed for many hours what had occurred at the Al-Rashid restaurant, but they still came back to the same unanswerable questions.

*What was the meaning of the Arabic name 'Ibrahim' written by Graham in his own blood as he lay slumped on the table dying?*

*How did the two terrorists know that Jack and Graham were lunching at the restaurant, particularly when it was a last minute decision of Graham to go there?*

*Who was the tall Black man who called himself Tom Robinson?*

Leila had already discovered from friendly American informants that there was no Tom Robinson employed as a civilian in the US military.

*Who had the terrorists been after, Jack or Graham or both of them?*

*How, without Graham at the British Embassy, were they to discover the location of the scrolls?*

Jack slept fitfully in Leila's second bedroom. His girlfriend had seen Leila on just one occasion, but she would have been horrified to think he was alone in the same apartment as such an attractive young woman. However, he was far too worried about finding the scrolls and horrified by his brush with death, to have any thoughts about trying to seduce the lovely Leila. In any case both he and Leila were totally professional and knew that, in their business, they must never become personally involved with each other. They were good friends and colleagues and that was where their relationship stood at that time. If either of them had any other ideas they were kept well concealed from each other.

Over breakfast they talked again. This time Jack came up with the idea of trying to place themselves in the position of the British.

'The SIS have lost an important operative,' he exclaimed, as much to himself as to Leila. 'If we were the SIS what would we do in the circumstances, given the desperation everyone has to get their hands on the scrolls?'

'Well,' Leila said, 'if I was the SIS I would be flying in somebody fairly senior to collect the scrolls. And they would have to accompanied by the one person who knows exactly where they are-your friend and my friend Sergeant Blackburn.'

'Exactly,' Jack agreed. 'And where would two such visitors to Baghdad stay?'

'My guess is the British Embassy. They wouldn't risk putting Craig Blackburn in a hotel. He could easily be recognised by visiting British Army personnel from the South.'

'Even at the Embassy,' he continued, 'the same danger exists. Remember, he is supposed to be dead.'

'So they will keep him under wraps until they have organised the trip South and he will almost certainly be disguised,' Leila replied.

'Right,' answered Jack. 'I dare not visit the Embassy. The Iraqi guy Hamid Ashraf, with whom I registered would certainly recognise me. In fact there are far too many people in this town who would now recognise me, including the police inspector Yacoub and the American who called himself Tom Robinson.'

'Ok,' Leila replied, 'I will have to try and follow up the possibility of Craig being at the British Embassy. I think I may have an American friend who could help. After all, I am an American citizen'

'Now,' Jack said, 'can we return to the name Ibrahim? Do you think that was the name of one of the assassins?'

obably,' Leila replied, 'but I will try and find ut the names of the two terrorists. I do have good contacts with the Iraqi police. As far as they are concerned I am the American assistant to Professor Sa'id and I genuinely do wonder what has become of him.'

'Yes,' she continued, 'my first port of call will be to see the Inspector who contacted me last week regarding the disappearance of the Professor. Now what was his name? Ah yes Inspector Tailouni.'

Jack felt that he had become totally superfluous to this investigation. He had been sent to Iraq to find the scrolls and although, to the best of his knowledge, no one knew he was an Israeli, his cover was seriously compromised as a result of the shooting.

**King David Hotel, Jerusalem.**

The Israelis had pulled out of Gaza the previous year. This was a painful decision as it entailed the uprooting of large numbers of their own loyal citizens and repatriating them to temporary accommodation within Israel. From there it was hoped to re-settle these people, who had become pawns in the strategy of separating the Israeli population from the Palestinians. The evacuation had been decided upon by the then Prime Minister Ariel Sharon with a view to facilitating a two state solution and democratic elections for the entire Palestinian people. The evacuation had been achieved with much heartache, but no bloodshed. However, by the summer of 2006 it was evident that with the Palestinians having elected a government from the terrorist hard-line Hamas party, dedicated to the destruction of the entire state of Israel and the increasing daily toll of death and damage resulting from missiles being propelled into Israel from Gaza, that the policy of withdrawal had been a terrible mistake. A young Israeli soldier was kidnapped from their side of the border and taken into Gaza to be held captive. This was the last straw and the Israeli armed forces were ordered to take whatever measures were necessary to rescue the young soldier and to put a stop to the bombardment from within Gaza. All this had come to a head while the Rev. Bill Cooper was visiting. As a result, the meeting with the Palestinian President was cancelled. It was considered, both by the Mossad and by his own Security people, to be far too dangerous for him to make the trip to Ramallah. It was probably not the wisest of ideas even in a relatively peaceful environment, given the Rev. Bill's well-publicised support for Israel and his uncomplimentary comments about Islam. Now, with the serious and escalating problems in Gaza, the trip to Ramallah would have been nothing short of madness.

Like most fanatics the Minister was no coward. He knew he was in the midst of a crisis, but he had allocated a month of his time to his stay in Israel and he was determined to see this through. In any case the information he had received from Iraq intrigued him.

The return call from Yossi, his contact in the Mossad, came just before dinner.

'Hello, Bill, you called. What can I do for you?' Yossi's voice came over the phone. He had developed a deep and understandable dislike for the Minister, but this had to be disguised both because the Rev. Bill was an honoured guest in Israel and because he had the means to destroy Yossi's career.

'We need to talk privately,' Bill replied gruffly, dispensing with all the niceties of the conversation. He was sure that with the information he held on the Mossad man, he could simply give out orders and they would be obeyed. 'That is impossible,' Yossi replied. 'You know we are in the middle of a crisis in Gaza and there is no chance of me taking the time to come to Jerusalem to see you.'

This made sense to the Minister who then suggested in a friendlier manner that maybe they could meet somewhere near where Yossi worked in the Negev desert.

Yossi tried every possible reason and excuse to avoid the meeting, but in the end agreed to meet the Rev. Bill in a small café on the Southern outskirts of Beersheba.

Had he known the real reason for the request for the meeting he would have even invoked the name of his boss, Ash, to say that he was under orders not to leave the secret headquarters. Yossi however, suspected that the reason for Bill's required meeting would have some connection with trying to obtain inside information regarding Gaza. He decided therefore, that as long as he was not involved in a long absence from the base he would try to humour this man who held so much power over him.

A Bedouin called Ismail ran the Café Yarok. It was really nothing more than a truck- stop and its most popular fare consisted of Humus and Pita, a variety of salads, Coca-Cola and thick strong Arabic coffee. Ismail had served in the Israel Border Police in his younger days and had cut a fine and distinguished figure in his uniform. Now he was back in his old environment, not far from the Bedouin tent in which he had been born. He shared his birthday with the State of Israel, May 15th 1948, but despite his casual appearance in jeans and t-shirt and his close-cropped beard, he still carried himself with a military air and appeared at least ten years younger than his fifty-eight years.

Apart from truck drivers on their way South to Eilat, the café had become popular with Israelis from Beersheba and points further North. Secret business meetings and assignations were often conducted there, well away from the various parties' normal haunts. The Café Yarok could not be described as elegant or fashionable, but it had its own unique atmosphere.

His visitors rarely surprised Ismail. Today, however, the two men seated at a quiet table to the rear of the establishment intrigued him. One man was obviously American. Not an American Jew however. With his long white hair and goatee beard he looked like one of those Southern Baptist Ministers. The other man was an Israeli, a smart young man in his early thirties. Ismail wondered why the young man had not been re-called to the Army in view of the trouble in Gaza. The news from the North was equally disturbing and Ismail had just heard on the radio of the murder of a number of Israeli soldiers just South of the Lebanese border and the kidnapping of the two surviving members of their patrol by the Hizb'ulla, who had returned to Lebanon with their prize captures. Ismail was a Sunni Muslim and had little or no sympathy for the Shi'a militia. Israel had been good to him and to his family and his loyalty was to the State. However, the condition of the people in Gaza distressed him. If only they could see the benefits they would have from making peace with the Israelis. They had been robbed blind for years by Arafat and his henchman of Al Fattah and now, after electing Hamas to power, once the Israelis had voluntarily withdrawn from their occupation, the ordinary people were paying the price for the belligerent attitude of Hamas towards Israel. Ismail knew exactly why Hamas had been elected. They were aggressive and fanatical, but they were also honest and unlike Al Fattah they seemed to care about the Palestinian people. Hamas just did not seem to understand, Ismail often thought, that however good their plans for social welfare were, unless they ceased to be on a war footing with Israel the ordinary Arab people would never have a decent life.

To the surprise and concern of his security men the Rev. Bill Cooper had insisted on walking alone from the dusty desert car park at the rear of the café. It had taken a few moments for the Rev. Bill to find Yossi as his eyes adjusted to the dark café after the brilliant gleaming light of the sun-lit desert outside. However, there he was, waiting for him at the rear of the somewhat musty establishment. The Minister could not help but approve the Mossad man's choice of location, quiet and away from the prying eyes of the curious multitude. As soon as they were seated Yossi ordered two Cokes and the Rev. Bill began the conversation.

'Don't you guys ever get any peace. You withdrew from Gaza and now Hamas are lobbing rockets at you from there. And have you heard the news on the radio?' he continued. 'The Hizb'ulla have killed some of your soldiers inside the Israel border and kidnapped another two poor boys.'

'Yes,' Yossi nodded grimly. His youngest brother was stationed in the North. He was only nineteen and Yossi was worried for his safety.

'Look,' the Minister continued. 'I am sure that with all that is going on you do not wish to indulge in chitchat about the situation. I care about Israel too, as you know,' he reminded Yossi. 'The sooner you can get back to work, the better. We are both on the same side.'

*So he does not want to question me about Gaza,* Yossi surmised. *Then what does he want?*

The Rev. Bill decided on a full frontal approach. He had Yossi in the palm of his hand so why pussyfoot around?

'Why is Jack in Iraq?' he enquired as casually as if he was asking the time of day.

Yossi was shocked and horrified. How could this American Minister know of Jack or of his movements?

Yossi tried to play for time.

'Who is Jack?' he replied.

'You know quite well who Jack is,' came the reply. 'He is one of your guys and he is in Iraq. The question is why?'

How on earth had the Rev. Bill got hold of this information? Was he bluffing? Did he have even more information? Why was he interested?

Then came an even greater shock.

'I guess he is after the scrolls,' the Minister muttered, almost as if he was thinking aloud.

Now Yossi was thoroughly rattled. How had the American obtained this top-secret information? He certainly could not have obtained reports about the scrolls from anyone in the Mossad. Yossi was sure of that. He could not see either the Brits or the Jordanian prince being in contact with Bill. As for the handful of Iraqis who knew the scrolls even existed, the Rev. Bill would be the last person on earth that they would confide in. And then it occurred to him that his presence at the café was compromising him further. If there were ever to be an investigation into how a Baptist Minister had obtained such sensitive security information, he would be the main suspect.

'Look Bill,' Yossi countered. 'I don't know what you are talking about. I don't know who Jack is. I think it is highly unlikely that anyone I know would be in Iraq. It is a dangerous place for everyone, especially Israelis. And as for the scrolls - what scrolls?'

'Sorry Yossi,' the Minister replied. 'I thought we were friends and friends don't have secrets from each other. You know I would never harm Israel. So come on. I don't want to be nasty - is Jack after the scrolls - yes or no!'

Yossi decided to continue with his bluff.

'I just do not know what you are talking about. All kinds of terrible problems are developing here in Israel and you are wasting my time with talk of some guy called Jack and scrolls!' Yossi made to rise, proffered his hand and continued,

'See you soon Bill.'

The Minister suddenly looked menacing.

'If you leave now without answering my questions, I will be forced to consider it a very unfriendly act. And you know what will happen next; a quick call to your boss, Ash. He will be really interested in a couple of the little incidents that occurred on your American visit. I would say that would be the end of your career and you might well be locked up for betraying your country. All I want to know is what is in the scrolls. I know some British soldier found them and buried them. I know he photographed them first. I know you guys know what they say. And I even know that they have something to do with a Caliph called An-Nasir. So all I want to know is what did this An-Nasir write in the scrolls.'

Yossi was beaten. How the Preacher knew so much was impossible to conjecture. But he did. Yossi decided that his only way out of this situation was to give the briefest of brief outlines about the scrolls. After all, he convinced himself, Bill was a good and close friend of Israel.

'Ok,' he began. 'You already know most of the story, but the subject of what is written in the scrolls is dynamite. You must promise me, as a man of God, that you would never divulge or use the information I am about to give you.'

The Rev. Bill looked sincere and contrite.

'You can rely on me,' he replied. 'I would never, ever do anything that would hurt Israel.'

'The scrolls contain the promise of the Sunni Caliph of Baghdad, An-Nasir, some thousand years ago, to help to re-establish a Jewish kingdom here in the Holy Land.

This would be in return for financial support from world Jewry in his fight with the Crusaders and the Shi'a Muslims.'

'There you have it,' Yossi continued breathlessly. 'Now you can see what would happen, if that information ever went public. It would really be best if you forgot all about it.'

Now it was the turn of the Rev. Bill to be shocked.

'Wow,' he exclaimed in a most un-ministerial way. 'But why don't you guys want to publicise this. It is another title deed to this land. Sure, your main title deeds are from the bible; then all your history here and the Balfour Declaration. But this beats the Balfour Declaration by a thousand years. And comes from a Muslim Prince.'

'But don't you see,' Yossi explained. 'There would be open war between the Shi'a and the Sunni and this would spread to all parts of the world, where Muslims live.'

'What is wrong with that?' the Rev. Bill asked. 'Let them slaughter each other while the Jews and Christians look on. Then maybe there would be no more terrorism, no more insurgents, no more violence, no more 9/11s or 7/7s and we could all live in peace.'

'Sorry Bill,' Yossi tried to explain. He had a horrible feeling that the Minister would see it that way. 'The Shi'a would not only attack the Sunni in more moderate countries like Jordan, but they would also attack us. We already have the President of Iran, a Shi'a, demanding our destruction.'

'At the same time,' Yossi continued, 'the moderate Sunni countries like Egypt and Jordan would attack us to try and convince their people that An-Nasir was way out of line and that, like all good Muslims they considered Israel to be a blot on the face of an Islamic Middle East.'

The Rev. Bill considered this and replied.

'I think you are wrong, but I promised to keep this a secret and a secret it will remain. That is unless something major happens to change the situation.'

And of course something major did happen, but not in the way the Rev. Bill had anticipated. The new outrage from Lebanon was the final straw for Israel. The Israelis had pulled out of Southern Lebanon some years earlier so that they could not be accused of occupying the territory of their Northern neighbour with all its attendant problems. However, instead of the Lebanese Army moving in to fill the vacuum, Hizb'ulla had filled it. They had continued to provoke Israel with rocket attacks, but not enough, or so they thought, to cause Israel to take action. However, now in 2006 they had entered Israel sovereign territory, murdered and kidnapped members of the Israeli army and Israel had had enough. The army, navy and air force were mobilised in an attempt to smash Hizb'ulla once and for all. This proved to be an impossible task, but a month later there could be no doubt that the Shi'a terrorist group had sustained substantial damage in the ensuing conflict. Sadly, but inevitably, this was at the expense of the lives of many Lebanese and Israeli civilians. Those civilians who had survived death or injury in the war had been forced to flee the war zones of Southern Lebanon and Northern Israel to safer areas of their respective countries.

As soon as the Rev. Bill Cooper realised that Israel was in a full-scale war situation he returned to the USA. He felt that he could help his Israeli friends far more effectively from there. In Israel he would have been a guest who would have been constantly in need of attention, if not protection. Back home he was able to maintain a constant barrage of press statements and organise meetings of his faithful to show the high level of vocal support that American Christians could give to their Israeli friends.

However, despite all this activity the Rev. Bill had certainly not forgotten about the last conversation he had had with Yossi. The scrolls were constantly on his mind as he tried to decide how best to use the information. He had made Yossi a promise, but he was seeking desperately for an excuse to break it. He was well aware of the conflagration that could result from the misuse of the Baghdad Declaration, but he longed to deal a hammering blow to Islam, as long as it could be achieved without damaging Israel and the USA. Unfortunately, the more he considered this the more the situation seemed to be impossible.

Jack had been called back to Israel and the Mossad had been obliged to place the matter of the scrolls on the back burner until an effective cease fire was organised with Hizb'ulla. Israel was insisting that the Lebanese army and the United Nations should police the area of the conflict. It remained to be seen how effectively they could control Hizb'ulla.

By September 2006, with the conflict over, at least for the time being, plans could have been made for Jack to return to Iraq. If only the Mossad could discover where in that vast country the scrolls were hidden. Leila had remained in Baghdad, but all of her inquiries had so far been totally unsuccessful.

## The 'Safe House.'

The 'safe-house' used by the SIS to domicile Craig during the Israel-Hizb'ulla war was not really a house at all. It was a series of large apartments in a block also used to house resident members of the British Intelligence community. It had a large paved area at the front that was protected by a high fence and security gates. The building itself was modern and unpretentious and most importantly it was located within the 'Green Zone' of Al Mansour. Craig had been taken there when James Smyth had been recalled to London during the recent conflict. James had left strict instructions with his SIS operatives that Craig was on no account to leave the apartment. However Craig had suffered more than enough imprisonment and although wishing to keep out of sight as much as possible, he was desperate to at least be able to smell the cooler evening air of Baghdad after sunset.

*What the hell,* he thought. *If I don't exist in the eyes of the British army, I can hardly be disciplined for failing to obey orders.*

Most of this last month he had been in the company of one of the rota of SIS men detailed to ensure that he stayed out of sight. The SIS was far more concerned by the prospect of Craig being recognised by visiting Army personnel than any other danger to his person. He had become a problem for the British Security Services at least until he could leave Baghdad and make the journey to where the scrolls were located.

His opportunity to escape, if only to savour the world outside the building, came during the second week of September. The duty SIS man had failed to show and it eventually transpired that the unfortunate man had ventured too near to a suicide bomber and had met an instant and horrible death. The SIS operative, who was scheduled to be relieved, was desperate to meet up with friends at his apartment nearby. They would be waiting outside and would represent a gift of a target to terrorists. You did not hang around the streets in Baghdad if you valued your life.

'Look Jack,' he had said. 'I think I know you well enough by now to trust you for just half an hour not to leave this suite. Remember, we will both be for the high jump if you are recognised.'

Craig smiled sweetly and nodded. The sooner the SIS man left, the better. Loneliness and lack of exercise had driven him to desperation. As soon as the SIS man was out of the way he put on his jacket, turned up the collar and pulled on a woolly hat. That was the only headgear he had possessed since the time when the Israelis had rescued him from the house of the Professor. They had insisted that he change out of his British army uniform and into non-descript civilian clothing, which they had supplied, before boarding the American helicopter. While in captivity he had also grown a beard which he felt would help him to merge into the general look of the population in the Baghdad street. That was assuming anyone would be out at night in such a dangerous city.

Carefully he opened the door to what had become both his home and his prison over the last few weeks. He slowly descended the wide staircase from the first floor landing. It was evening and he was sure that only a small number of personnel would be on duty in the lobby of the building. When he had arrived at the apartment block he had noticed that there was a security man on reception and a further two men guarding the door. That had also been at night and Craig was initially relieved to see the same manning level. Then there was the outer area where soldiers and security personnel would be positioned right up to the outer security gate. Finally out on the street there would be the American and Iraqi police detailed to guard all foreign buildings in the city. The Safe House may be in the so-called Green Zone, but even here a lone pedestrian was in considerable danger.

Standing just out of sight at the bottom of the staircase, Craig started to consider all of this and to realise the absolute madness of the course of action he had commenced. Although he was desperate for fresh air and exercise he realised that there was just no way that he could escape in this manner. All the security might have been set up to keep out the many dangerous people on the outside, but it was also certainly going to keep Craig a prisoner on the inside.

Just as he was about to return reluctantly and sadly climb the stairs back to the apartment, he heard the sounds of a number of people entering the lobby. There were at least six men in the party and one by one they were being processed through the final check point by the two security men at the lobby door. Two of the visitors looked like British SIS men, but obviously senior to the men who were detailed to guard him. The other four were Arabs. All four wore the distinctive Keffiyeh of the Jordanian army. Craig was intrigued. Why were four Jordanians visiting a British Safe-House in Baghdad at eight o'clock on a Thursday evening? Two of the men looked vaguely familiar. And then it struck him in a flash of horror that one of them was the Jordanian Prince who he had met in Amman after his escape from the villa of the Professor. *Now what was his name*, he puzzled. And then he remembered: Prince Jamal ibn Musa.

It was the other familiar looking Jordanian who he felt he should have been able to identify. He was wearing his Keffiyeh loosely, in the style of the Druze and had a full beard that virtually obscured his face. Craig could not see his eyes, but there was something about the way he moved, his body language, the way he held his head, the way he walked, that made Craig feel that he had seen this man many times before. He stood there just out of sight from the lobby, peering round the corner to try and ascertain which apartment the Jordanians might be visiting. Craig was intrigued as to why the Prince would be there and even more intrigued to discover who the other man might be. And then he was startled by a voice behind him saying,

'And what might you be doing here?'

It was the SIS guard returned from his half hour away and horrified to find Craig's suite empty. He had been frantic to discover what had become of his charge and had been descending the stairs somewhat noisily when he saw Craig standing motionless on the bottom stair. All Craig's military training had deserted him. It was incredible that he should not have heard the SIS man coming down the stairs behind him, but his concentration was entirely on the visitors. Once the SIS man spoke the sound reverberated in the almost empty marble floored lobby and all six visitors turned anxiously to identify the origin of the sudden sound. And then with a shock Craig recognised the other visitor. It was Professor Sa'id. Recovering himself, Craig turned to confront the SIS man whose confidence in him he had so severely shaken.

'I was desperate for some evening air,' he stuttered. 'I was just about to ask permission from the security guard for a brief walk just outside the door when the visitors arrived.'

'Sorry Craig,' the SIS man replied, deeply relieved to have recovered his charge. 'I really am surprised at you. You know damn well that you could have been recognised by one of the soldiers outside and then we would both have been in big trouble. Come on, back to the room before anyone realises who you are and where you are.'

Unbeknown to him, the damage had already been done. Craig had been recognised, but not by British personnel. Both Prince Jamal ibn Musa and the Professor had seen him and now knew where he was and they already knew that he was the only living person who could reliably locate the scrolls.

Craig had great difficulty in sleeping that night. He had received a thorough scolding from the SIS man guarding him. Craig knew he was totally in the wrong. Even if he had managed to get outside and on to the street, he knew full well that the course of action would have been nothing less than suicidal. He was frustrated and bitter. To be captured by insurgents was one thing, but to be held as a prisoner by his own countrymen was totally intolerable. The knowledge that none of those near and dear to him even knew he was still alive was a heavy enough burden and then there was the matter of those 'bloody' scrolls. Taking the back route through the desert was the worst mistake of his entire life. Indeed he knew that it could still prove to be fatal for him. His life according to the British army had already been forfeited. And then, worst of all, he was personally responsible for the deaths of his three comrades. And now, the Iraqi Professor and the Jordanian prince knew where he was. Given the slightest opportunity they would re-capture him and force him to take them to the cave where the scrolls were hidden.

The next few days were an agony of mental torture for the British sergeant. The SIS men now guarded him more zealously than ever. They never left his side. Even when his troubled mind did allow him to snatch a few minutes of sleep he would awake to find one of them sitting quietly and patiently in his room. Before they had chatted with him and treated him as a friend and almost a colleague. Now they saw him as a troublesome burden that interfered with their more usual duties. He was no longer trusted. That was until James Smyth returned from London.

### Nashville. Tennessee

The Rev. Bill Cooper was on tour again. With the situation on the Lebanese/Israel border returning to its more normal precarious semi-calm, the Minister was back in his familiar role of spreading the Gospel according to the holy words of Saint Bill. As usual he was preaching a heady and often dangerous mixture of religion and politics to the bands of followers who surfaced in every town he visited. Nashville was no different to the others and on the evening of September 23rd which happened to be the start of the Jewish New Year, while the Jews were praying earnestly in their Synagogues throughout the world for peace and forgiveness for their sins, the Rev. Bill was also praying with some ten thousand members of his Church for peace, but peace on his own terms. And those terms included many messages that could hardly be deemed to be conducive to international and inter-religious tranquillity. As usual, he blessed his own flock and the Jewish people, especially those in Israel. As usual he heavily criticised other Christian denominations; especially the Roman Catholic Church. And as usual he had hard and aggressive comments to make about the followers of Mohammed, be they Shi'a or Sunni Muslims. His words on the subject of Islam were even more poisonous than usual. The Minister wholly cursed the religion and its adherents, speaking of the Prophet and of his Koran in the most scathing of terms.

After the long diatribe he met up with his security adviser and worldwide spy, Henry Roberts, also known as Tom Robinson. Henry had also returned to the USA with the outbreak of the Hizb'ulla war. In common with the Israelis, the Jordanian Prince and the Iraqi Professor Sa'id, he had been totally unable to discover either the location of the scrolls or anyone among the British personnel in Baghdad who was prepared to impart such information.

The meeting in Nashville between the Rev. Bill and Henry was of little use to the Minister, but as Henry had been a good and trusted servant of the Church for some years now, Bill decided to tell him about the contents of the scrolls and what Yossi had explained to him about the incredible danger, as the Israelis saw it, surrounding any leakage of the information contained in the scrolls to the world media.

The conversation was almost identical to that between Bill and Yossi just a few weeks earlier in the Café Yarok outside Beersheba. The only difference was that Henry took the line that Bill had taken during the previous conversation and recommended releasing the story to bolster up the legitimacy of the State of Israel and to deal a hammering blow to Islam by ensuring a worldwide civil war between the two main Muslim groups.

The Minister found himself in the unusual role of urging caution and explaining that their friends in Israel and the Christian countries would also suffer from such a major conflagration.

'My dear friend Bill,' Henry finally said. 'You know I always look upon you as more than just a leader and spiritual adviser. You have been a good friend to me and I always listen to your words of wisdom and act upon them. Forgive me if I say that I believe we are missing a God-given opportunity here to destroy the religion that we both know has caused so much human suffering, particularly in the last few years.'

Henry's hatred of Islam was possibly even bitterer than that of his leader and mentor. He had been brought up in a poor district in the Bronx and was the oldest of five children, all boys. By the age of sixteen his brother Eugene had become a hardened and persistent petty criminal. He was then jailed for larceny and while serving his sentence he had met two Pakistani brothers who had persuaded him to convert to Islam. They had told him that the Christianity of his parents was an alien religion for people of colour, brown or black, and that his true spiritual home should be with them at the Mosque. By the time he was paroled he had become a fanatical Muslim and after a spell in a Pakistani Madrassa he was sent over the border to Afghanistan to learn the theory and application of Jihad. Eugene or Ismail as he was now known, was then trained as a Shahid, a suicide bomber. Before he could apply his new skills however, and destroy the lives of innocent people together with his own, the family were told in a mysterious letter that dropped through their letterbox one day, that an accident with explosions in his training camp had abruptly ended his career and his short and unhappy life. Henry was broken-hearted when he eventually discovered what had become of Eugene and his hatred for the religion of Mohammed was therefore very personal.

As soon as their conversation ended with a hitherto unprecedented disagreement, three of the Rev. Bill's bodyguards were waiting to escort him back to his hotel.

The large car park that fronted the stadium where he had spoken to the gathered multitude of his supporters just an hour earlier was now almost empty and his limousine was brought as close as possible to the doorway from which he emerged. It was then that the one staccato shot rang out and the Rev. Bill sank instantly to the ground. The beloved leader, the prophet of the Church of the Second Coming was dead.

**Somewhere in Southern England.**

James Smyth had been due to return to Baghdad a few days earlier. Had he arrived when he originally planned, Craig's little escapade, that had exposed him to the Professor and the Prince, would probably not have occurred. As it was, the reason for his delay was because at the highest level within the SIS, the decision had been taken to discuss the scrolls with the Mossad. They needed to know and to be sure that there really was a complete identity of purpose with the Israelis on the subject of the scrolls. The SIS had a plan and a meeting with the Mossad was the only way of seeing if it was viable.

Secret contacts between allied security establishments often occurred, but usually informally and at lower levels. On this occasion an invitation was issued through top-secret channels and at the highest levels. The coded message arrived at the Mossad and just one day later Ash and Jack arrived at Heathrow. One hastens to add that they did not travel on an El Al flight. Their route took them via Istanbul and the two businessmen, one 'Turkish' and the other 'English,' were quickly whisked away to a secret destination where the discussions were to take place.

The senior SIS officers would have also liked to have included the Hashemite Kingdom of Jordan in the talks, but had long since discovered that Prince Jamal ibn Musa had his own agenda. Curiously he had failed to keep any other member of the Royal Family or the Jordanian government informed even of the existence of the scrolls, let alone their content. The two parties to the secret talks, now taking place, discussed this disconcerting silence on the part of the Prince. Both the British and the Israelis found his behaviour more than a little worrying. Prince Jamal had first heard of the scrolls from the Israeli Prime Minister. That was a lamentable breach of security. As a result the Mossad was now intent on keeping Yigal Shomroni as much out of the picture as they dared, but he was their boss as head of state. The Prime Minister frequently asked for reports and up-dates on the situation with the scrolls, but the lack of information on their location enabled the Mossad to issue reports of little or no progress in answer to these requests.

Prince Jamal was well known both in Britain and Israel. He was considered to be a voice of moderation in the Arab and Islamic world. Now it soon transpired that he had not only failed to pass on important information to his own government, but also that neither the UK nor the Israeli security services had heard anything from him or of him for over a month.

'I have to tell you my dear friend Ash,' James commented once the two Israelis were settled at the large mahogany table in the Conference room at the secret establishment, 'I am extremely worried about the way this whole affair is going. Prince Jamal was behaving totally out of character and now he has disappeared. The Professor seemed to have perished when his home in Iraq burned down, but we have no confirmation of this.'

He continued the catalogue of disturbing events. 'One of our best operatives in Baghdad was shot dead just a few weeks ago.'

Ash and Jack nodded sympathetically. An exchange of useful information was one thing, but to admit that Jack was with Graham when he was shot would only serve to damage the warm relationship that existed between the two security services. In the shady world of the international intelligence services all information, even among friends, was only transmitted on the basis of 'need to know.'

'What information do you have about that?' Ash enquired. 'Do you think that what happened to your man had any connection to the matter we are here to discuss today?'

'Impossible to say,' James replied. 'He had some mysterious companion with him who we have been unable to find or identity. Graham was shot by two Iraqi terrorists and they in turn were shot dead by another unidentified man, a black American at another table in the café.'

'There are far too many loose ends in this whole situation,' James continued.

'Well,' Ash said after a momentary pause in conversation. 'You asked us to come over to discuss the scrolls. How can we help?'

'I am sure you know that there is only one living person who can lead us accurately to the scrolls,' James volunteered.

'Yes,' Ash replied, 'that much we know. He is one of your guys. A British Sergeant originally stationed at Basra.'

'What I must ask you now is what would be the Israeli position if the scrolls were found and made public,' James replied. 'We know that you are aware of what they say from your agent Leila in Iraq. That much Prince Jamal told our Ambassador to Jordan at the time.'

'To put it bluntly we are terrified when we consider the consequences of the Shi'a Muslims learning about them,' Ash answered with a look of grave concern. 'There would be outright war between the Sunni and the Shi'a, between Iran and Saudi Arabia, civil war in Lebanon and Syria, Jordan would be attacked as would Egypt. It would not end there. Battles would flare up in British, French and other European cities with large Muslim populations and even the USA would not escape serious trouble. As for Israel, we would be caught in the crossfire of a war beyond anything hitherto seen and that includes World War Two,' he finished lamely.

'I think I knew you guys well enough to expect that this would be your answer. So you agree? First we must find the scrolls and then destroy them,' James continued.

'Absolutely,' Ash agreed and noted that Jack was nodding furiously at his side.

'Ok,' James continued. 'Now that is clearly understood I can tell you that I have clearance at the highest level to disclose to you the location of the scrolls. However we want it understood that this information is for your eyes and ears only. Do I have your undertaking as senior members of the Mossad that what I am about to tell you will remain within the provenance of just the three of us. The only other person with this knowledge, as you know, is our Sergeant Craig Blackburn.'

Both Ash and Jack nodded gravely.

'You have our word,' Ash promised.

'Have you ever heard of the cave of Ibrahim?' James enquired.

The two Israelis shook their heads.

'It is a cave in the desert some thirty miles to the North of Basra. It is considered by local legend to be where Abraham or Ibrahim as the Arabs call him, stopped off to rest, on his journey from Chaldea to what we now call Syria,' James explained.

'We have a good idea from Craig where the cave is located, but only Craig knows where he re-buried the scrolls within the cave.'

'Ok,' Ash replied. 'Now how do we help?'

James turned to address Jack directly.

'I believe you met Craig, when you rescued him from the Professor's house in Iraq.'

Jack nodded, beginning to suspect that he knew where this was going.

'Could you work with him?' James enquired.

'Yes, sure.' Jack replied.

James turned back to face Ash.

'What I have to suggest is virtually unheard of, certainly in the SIS and I suspect in the Mossad. However, we are dealing with an unprecedented threat to the way of life of us all.'

'If you agree Ash, we would like to borrow Jack and return him to Iraq as a British soldier. We would then arrange an expedition by Craig and Jack to the cave to locate and destroy the scrolls once and for all.'

Ash turned to Jack.

'This is way beyond the call of duty. I cannot order you to undertake such a dangerous expedition. You will be working directly for the British, but there can be no doubt that this proposal is in the vital interest of the State of Israel.'

'Having said that,' Ash continued, 'you will be on your own. There is no way Israel or the Mossad could help you if you get into any kind of difficulty while involved in this operation.'

'You will however have the full backup of the SIS and the area concerned is within our sphere of operation,' James gently and reassuringly added.

Jack grimaced.

'Ok, I will do it,' he said.

'That is just the answer I expected from you,' Ash replied.

'Right,' Jack said with a sigh. 'When do we start?'

**Israel.**

The Israeli newspapers were full of news regarding the United Nations resolution on South Lebanon. There were also long reports and endless articles assessing the success and/or failure of the campaign. However, the assassination of an American Baptist Minister still made headlines. Had it been anyone other than the Rev. Bill Cooper a paragraph on an inner page would have sufficed. However, the Rev. Bill Cooper was not anyone. He was the most spectacular, vocal and committed friend Israel had ever had in the Christian world. True, he was so extreme in his loyalty and in his views that he was often an embarrassment. Nevertheless he had made headlines for most of his adult life and he certainly made headlines in the USA and Israel by the manner of his death. Who had killed him? Why had he been murdered? Was it his support for Israel, come what may, or his support for the American campaigns in Iraq and Afghanistan? Was it his avowed hatred of Islam or his dislike of Roman Catholicism? There were plenty of candidates for the job of assassin and even more theories.

So far the American Police and the FBI had been unable to identify anyone who might have done the deed. Often in investigations like this there is a dearth of suspects. In this case however, there were far too many. There may have been thousands of people who claimed to be his friends, but there was absolutely no shortage of enemies either. Two witnesses claimed to have seen a tall black man behaving suspiciously at the other end of the car park, but the police eventually decided that he was probably just a local man looking for opportunities to burgle parked cars and who was leaving after the rally had ended.

Henry Roberts found himself at the centre of all these investigations. He had been standing next to the Rev. Bill when the snipers bullet had made a neat little hole in the centre of the Minister's forehead. He was also the last person to have spoken at any length to Rev. Cooper. The investigators wanted to know what had been discussed; whether Bill had shown any sign of nervousness or appeared, to the slightest degree, to be apprehensive and whether he had mentioned that he had been threatened. Had he had an argument or even a fight with anyone? To all these questions and many more, Henry could answer with conviction, in the negative. However, both the Police and the FBI returned almost daily with more questions and then when they checked his itinerary and realised that the Minister had recently been in Israel, they even involved the CIA. All of this was to no avail.

Unbeknown to Henry, the CIA had quickly contacted the Mossad and they had ultimately been routed through on a secure line to Ash. He had been very concerned when he had originally been notified of Bill's murder, but could see no connection to Israel and the Mossad other than the very obvious hatred he had shown to the world of Islam. After the phone call he immediately called Yossi in to his office and told him of the call from the CIA.

Yossi did not know whether to laugh or to cry when he had heard of the death. The Rev. Bill had a terrifying hold over Yossi and could have ended the young Mossad man's career with just one short phone call to Ash. In addition to being dismissed ignominiously from the service, Yossi could well have been jailed as a result of his passing to the Minister state secrets regarding the Scrolls. The assassination of Rev. Cooper lifted a huge weight from Yossi's mind, but at the same time, although he disliked the man, he had never wished him dead.

**USA.**

The Elders of the Church of the Second Coming had called an emergency meeting within hours of their leader and spiritual guide's death. As these worthy men gathered from all parts of the United States, mainly from the South, they were in deep shock. Who could conceivably have wanted to destroy the life of a man who had achieved so much for Christianity and for the cause of the Second Coming?

They had a serious problem. The Rev. Bill had no nominated successor. He had imagined himself to be virtually indestructible or at least to have the strength and determination to soldier on into a distinguished old age. In his own mind he often imagined when his days were eventually to draw to a close a resurrection for himself alongside his saviour Jesus; he had been preaching this kind of thing for so long that he actually began to believe it himself.

The Elders of the Church consisted of men considered by their colleagues to be of great integrity and deep religiosity. As to the almost magical ability to spellbind huge crowds in the manner of their founder, this was completely absent in the group. They were followers not leaders. The Chairman for the meeting was the Rev. Johnny Winchester. He was a good and able man and a sincere preacher at his own branch of the church in Houston. However he was no leader and certainly no orator. As a result of the complete absence of this kind of talent within the group, it was initially decided that they would all continue to look after their own local congregations. However, huge rallies such as those previously addressed by their dead leader would now have to await the arrival of a new Shepherd for their combined flocks. Where this shepherd would be found was something they decided, after hours of agonised debate, to leave to the Almighty to provide, when the time was ripe. The only other possible way might be to tour in groups and it was resolved to consider this proposal.

Henry Roberts as the head of the Church's security and a long-time confidante of the late minister had been invited to attend the meeting and he had been authorised to deal with further Police enquiries and the general administration on behalf of the Church. The Rev. Johnny Winchester ceremoniously passed to Henry the keys to Bill's private offices and safes and the meeting ended with a tearful prayer for the soul of their departed leader.

Henry lost no time in taking charge of the large and luxurious administration suite. His fervour for the church was only exceeded by his profound hatred for Islam. He was undoubtedly a sincere Christian, but more in the style of Oliver Cromwell than St Francis of Assisi. Had he been born an Englishman in the days of the Protectorate he would certainly have subscribed to the Cromwellian ethos of 'trust in God, but keep your powder dry.'

At first Henry hesitated to sit behind the huge carved walnut desk where he had, for so long, been accustomed to seeing his leader sitting. However, Henry would hardly have reached the upper echelons of the church without a reasonable degree of self-confidence. When all was said and done he was a black man from the wrong side of New York City. In fact, New Yorkers were few and far between in the Church of the Second Coming. Most of the senior positions were in the hands of White Southerners. Henry had been accustomed to occasionally allow his mind to drift back some thirty years when the sight of a New York black man or any other black man come to that, anywhere within the sacred portals of this organisation would have been unthinkable. As he settled himself in the late Rev. Bill's leather chair he considered the new situation that had so unexpectedly been thrust upon him. It was late evening and Henry quickly decided that whatever administrative work there was would have to wait for the following morning. Nevertheless, he felt, a quick look in the huge office safe would not go amiss before he returned to his hotel.

The safe was not expected to contain money. In these days of credit cards and electronic banking that would not be its purpose. There was however just $1,000 in the petty cash box, obviously for emergencies. That had no interest to Henry. He was known to be scrupulously honest and was well paid for his endeavours for the church in any case.

The other contents of the safe were such items as Insurance Policies and large numbers of CD master disks. These included recordings and DVDs of the Rev. Bill's lectures, all meticulously labelled. Then there were the system disks for the sophisticated computer system installed just last year. Finally and unexpectedly there was one large brown envelope marked with a 'Y.' It was unsealed. Henry's native curiosity drove him to lift the envelope from the safe and slide the contents out on to the desk. He sat down again and began to read a list of the contents of the numbered disks that the envelope had contained. 'Y at Rally,' he read and then 'Y at hotel.'

Who on earth was 'Y' Henry wondered and decided to place the second DVD in the computer drive.

It was a movie of a young man of Middle Eastern appearance in a hotel bedroom. The room looked familiar and Henry was sure, judging by the furnishings, that he must have visited a similar room in the same establishment. The man was a complete stranger to Henry and he watched, his curiosity thoroughly aroused, as this stranger settled himself down, glass in hand to watch TV. *What on earth did Bill want with this boring stuff?* Henry wondered. Then there was the sound of a buzzer off camera and the stranger arose, a little unsteadily and disappeared from view. Some thirty seconds later he was back in the frame and accompanied by a young woman. Henry thought that the woman looked familiar, but her scooped back hair and loose all-enveloping robe seemed strange and ill fitting. Then suddenly Henry realised that this was the woman who had caused a scandal that could have seriously damaged the church. Her name escaped him as the whole incident had occurred over two years ago. She was a senior clerical assistant in the organisation and supposedly a sincere committed Christian.

Then she had been discovered working as a Call Girl in the evenings. Bill had asked Henry to visit the woman to fire her and to ensure her silence. This proved unnecessary and Bill explained, before Henry had time to arrange the visit, that the Police Chief in the town was a member of the Church. He was as determined as Bill to keep the affair under wraps. Bill had also explained to Henry that he himself had spoken to the woman who was ashamed of her conduct and only wished to avoid adverse publicity for the Church and for herself.

The DVD seemed to be a film of the woman visiting one of her nocturnal clients. But why would Bill wish to keep the disk? The idea of the leader of his Church being a voyeur was surely unthinkable. Henry decided that he must see what happened next in the movie. He was a religious Christian, but the temptation to view a little more of the DVD was overwhelming. Up till that point the only sound had been from a TV set but now a conversation ensued between the woman and the man. Henry had a good ear for accents and quickly realised that the man had a strong, thick Israeli accent. He was slurring his words and appeared to be quite drunk. Henry knew lots of Israelis, but had never before encountered a drunken one. More conversation ensued and more drink was consumed, after which matters reached their logical conclusion with the two parties writhing together naked on the large hotel bed. The DVD ended with the man falling into a deep sleep and the woman quickly and silently dressing before slipping quietly out of the room.

*Was this evidence of the woman's past activities?* Henry wondered. However, the fact that the man was Israeli worried him. He right-clicked on the icon before ejecting the disk and was astonished to discover that the DVD had only been filmed in the late spring of that year. He knew it was at least two years since the woman had worked for the Church and he sensed that there was more to this story than just a film of a client being serviced by a Call Girl.

There was another film in the envelope and Henry decided to run this disk as well. The DVD proved to be a record of one of the Rev. Bill's rallies. This seemed to be nothing out of the ordinary until at the end the Minister introduced a visitor from Israel. Rev. Bill invited him to say a few words to the gathered multitude and when he arose to speak the camera zoomed in to show the same young man from the hotel bedroom that he had just watched cavorting with the prostitute.

It was now well after midnight, but Henry needed answers and he needed them immediately. He knew the date of the second DVD and he decided to check Bill's diary for evidence of a visiting Israeli. That proved to be an easy task. The man was known as Yossi and much to Henry's utter amazement he worked for the Mossad.

And then Henry found the carefully hand written notes of the Rev. Bill's last meeting with Yossi. He sat there mesmerised as he read over and over again the story of the scrolls that Bill referred to as the Baghdad Declaration. *This is heaven sent,* he decided. *Now we can remove the curse of Islam once*

*and for all. They will all be at each other's throats like
the pack of dogs they are.*

## Baghdad.
## The Safe House.

The young Englishman with a slight Manchester
accent, probably an army officer, his fellow
passengers quickly decided, descended from the
aircraft. He was whisked past security and
customs and under heavy guard, for his own
protection, deposited at the 'Safe House' as
speedily as the traffic would allow.

There, his SIS escorts guided him through the
various checks to the apartment occupied by the
officially late lamented (but still very much alive)
Sergeant Craig Blackburn. Craig had been
expecting the visitor and had been thoroughly
briefed by senior SIS personnel.

Jack and Craig had only met once before, but that
had been a very long meeting. It had started in the
Iraqi desert and finished the following day in the
home of the Jordanian, Prince Jamal ibn Musa.
The two young Mancunian men, although from
diverse ethnic and social backgrounds, had
immediately formed a bond of friendship. The
cement that firmly fixed this friendship was at
least in part, due to the fact that they both
supported Manchester City Football Club.
However, their world was turning on far, far
graver matters than football.

Craig desperately needed to talk to Jack privately.
He suspected that the apartment would probably
be bugged. When all was said and done it was an
SIS Safe House and must frequently have given

shelter to people that the British authorities could not have been sure they could trust. Since the escapade when he had left the apartment and had been discovered at the bottom of the stairs, he was never left alone. The SIS men who guarded him tried to be as companionable as possible, but he knew that they no longer considered him to be entirely reliable. In two days time James Smyth would arrive and after a thorough briefing he would be on his way with Jack to the Cave of Ibrahim. In the meantime he had to let Jack know that the occupants of another apartment in this self-same building were none other than Prince Jamal and the missing Professor Sa'id.

Craig had been delighted to welcome Jack and although he worked for the Mossad, the mere fact that he was there showed that the SIS trusted him. In the end he managed to write a note that he was able to give to Jack when their SIS guard had momentarily turned his back. Jack was there as a guest and as a member of a foreign elite Intelligence Agency and as such was not subject to the surveillance now being given to the British Sergeant. He simply retired to his bedroom and was shocked to discover what Craig had written. He had been told about the incident when Craig left the apartment and knew this was one of the reasons why he had been chosen to accompany Craig to the Cave. It was a strange turn of events when the senior British Intelligence Officer, James Smyth, had more confidence in an Israeli Mossad operative than in one of his own country's soldiers.

The crumpled note read:

*Prince Jamal and Professor Sa'id arrived here three days ago. I know they saw me and recognised me just as I recognised them. Who on earth authorised them to stay here I can't imagine? I am sure it was not James Smyth. He would want them both as far away from me as possible. I have not seen them since, so they may have left by now, but we all know what they are after, don't we? Now they are aware that I am here, I can't see them leaving in a hurry. I have not told the SIS about this as I am in enough trouble already for trying to get away from this apartment, if only for a break. Now you have arrived, even with the blessing of the SIS, the situation is even worse. For goodness sake, stay out of sight. Cheers, Craig.*

Jack read the note through twice, scarcely able to believe it. *So the Professor is alive!* He marvelled, *and why would Jordanian Prince Jamal accompany him here to a city where he was in such great danger, should he be recognised? What a prize that would be for the insurgents, if they were able to capture him!*

To stay in a hotel had been a bad mistake for Prince Jamal. His arrival with his retinue could hardly have been described as low key and news of the visit of any prominent personality would have been known in the wrong quarters within minutes. Just two days later a gun battle of serious proportions had occurred outside the hotel between members of the Iraqi security forces and a large group of terrorists who had managed to infiltrate the Al Mansour district. There was no doubt who they were after.

Prince Jamal had appealed to the British Ambassador in Iraq for protection. Baghdad was of course part of the large area of the country where the American military was assigned to help the fledgling Iraqi government to achieve a semblance of law and order. So far their efforts had met with little or no success. Gangs of insurgents from the two opposing religious groups were inflicting a daily carnage of horrific proportions on each other and on the vast majority of their fellow citizens who just longed to proceed with their lives in peace. Prince Jamal, like many Jordanians, always felt closer to the British than to the Americans. He and most of the senior members of the royal family were educated in England. The British Ambassador had quickly arranged for the Prince and his companions to be transferred to the Safe House.

The transfer had, of course, been arranged with British Security Service personnel, but apart from James Smyth the whole story of the scrolls was known only to a handful of senior members of the SIS echelons. The fact that HM Government was able to offer a safe haven to a member of the Royal family of a friendly country was more than sufficient to guarantee that Prince Jamal would be well looked after in the Safe House.

Professor Sa'id had been astonished that the Prince had been willing, nay determined to escort his old friend back to Baghdad.

'My dear friend,' the Professor had said when the Prince had suggested this course of action. 'My beloved city, Baghdad is one of the most dangerous cities on earth at the present time. It is dangerous for all Iraqis; it is even more dangerous for Europeans. The Iraqi Shi'a probably hate you, as a member of the Royal Hashemite family, almost as much as they hate the Israelis. Iraq is my country and I will return there alone.'

The Prince would have none of this. He was internationally known as a man of peace, but since he had heard about the scrolls and had seen the photographs that Craig had taken of the Arabic text, his whole attitude to life and to his place in the scheme of things had changed. This was why he had kept the news of the discovery of the scrolls to himself. Prince Jamal had always recognised that he was a fairly junior member of the Royal Dynasty. He considered it to be his duty to support his distant cousin, the King, and other members of the family and to use his own best endeavours to ensure that his country would be influential not only in the Middle East, but in the world family of nations. When he had first seen and read the text of the scroll he quickly realised the danger it posed to his country. However, he began to brood over the fact that the Caliph An Nasir had signed the scrolls. It was a fairly well guarded secret in Jordanian Royal circles that Jamal, on his mother's side was a direct descendant of that self-same Caliph. And were not the Caliphs of Baghdad descendants of the Prophet himself? Suddenly, from being a pragmatic fairly small part player on the international stage he felt that destiny was calling him; or rather the voice of his illustrious ancestor An Nasir was calling to him. He hardly slept and he had a fast growing obsession that he and he alone, could answer the call of the Caliph from a thousand years ago. He had to obtain the scrolls and he had to act on them. That meant making them known to an unsuspecting world. It also meant recognising the rights of the Israelis to their land. And most seriously of all it meant declaring the Shi'a Muslims to be usurpers and to have no place in the Islamic world.

At first, Prince Jamal appeared virtually unchanged to his associates, but he was now a man with a dream that could potentially become a nightmare for everyone else. In this waking dream, once he had destroyed the Shi'a he would, by popular acclaim be invited to rule over a suddenly and miraculously peaceful Iraq and become the greatest Caliph in history. This would be but a small step to his becoming the unchallenged leader of the entire Arab world. All of this was carefully concealed from his old friend the Professor and he absolutely insisted on accompanying him to Baghdad despite all the very real warnings of the dangers of making such a trip.

The Professor for his part could hardly have failed to notice the change in his Royal friend. However there was nothing he could do to dissuade the Prince from accompanying him and that is how the two men and their aides came to be in the British Safe House in Baghdad, when a world already beset with plenty of troubles could never have anticipated the potential for even more cataclysmic events that could emanate from within those four walls.

**Somewhere in the Negev Desert.**

'Hello,' said the friendly American voice over the telephone. 'My name is Henry Roberts and I am the administrator of the Church of the Second Coming. I am sure you are aware of the tragic death of our leader, the Rev. Bill Cooper?'

Ash knew who was calling him and only agreed to accept the call when he was assured that this man was now acting as virtual leader of the Church.

'Hello Mr Roberts,' Ash replied. 'I am deeply sorry to hear of the assassination of your Senior Minister.'

'What can I do for you?' he continued. 'I am sure you understand that any enquiries that your authorities wish to make must be transmitted through normal channels.'

Henry had anticipated this reply. He had not expected to be able to speak directly to any member of the Mossad let alone to a head of station such as Ash. However, the coded telephone number in one of Bill's diaries had led him straight to the fountainhead. Now he needed to somehow get in touch with Yossi.

'I believe you have an operative called Yossi in your team,' he ventured. 'I also believe he was the security liaison-officer who worked to ensure a safe and successful recent visit to your country by poor Bill Cooper.'

Then Henry had a brain wave.

'I am sure you will be pleased to know that the late Rev. Bill was so pleased with the security arrangements made by Yossi that he had left him a gift as a mark of appreciation.'

'I am afraid that no member of the Israel Security Services can accept gifts. We all do our work for the benefit of Israel and of its friends,' Ash explained.

'But this is a signed copy of the Old Testament and I am sure that such a good friend of Israel as our late leader would have been heart broken if such a small token of gratitude could not be accepted.'

Ash relented just as Henry hoped. He had more than enough to contend with. Arguing with someone whose motives appeared to be so completely innocent and transparent, about such a petty matter seemed to be totally irrelevant in the scheme of things.

'Ok,' Ash replied. 'I will get Yossi to call you. Can he get you on this number?'

'Sure,' Henry replied, 'and thanks.'

Half an hour later when Yossi came on duty Ash sent for him and told him to telephone Henry at once.

Yossi was of course far from happy to have to make contact with any member of the Church of the Second Coming. He feared the worst and his forebodings proved to be entirely justified.

With a heavy heart Yossi made the call. He had never met Henry, but Ash had told him that it was a small matter and one that would please him when he heard what this Henry had to say. Yossi suspected that the complete opposite would be the case.

Henry played the game like the professional he was.

'Hi, is this Yossi?' he enquired. 'My name is Henry Roberts. I am the chief security officer and temporary administrator for the Church of the Second Coming,' he explained when Yossi had confirmed his own identity.

'I am sure you know that our dear senior Minister, the Rev. Bill Cooper, was recently murdered,' he began.

Yossi was sure that he knew what was coming next.

'Yes, of course,' he answered. 'I was so very sorry to hear the news. How may I help you?'

'No, it is I who has good news for you. ' Henry replied. 'I have to tell you that the Rev. Bill had a gift for you as a token of appreciation for the way you had made arrangements for his recent trip to Israel.'

'Oh,' Yossi said, wondering what was coming next. 'That is very nice, but we are not allowed to accept presents for just doing our job.'

'It is ok,' Henry explained. 'The gift is a leather bound and signed copy of the Old Testament. Your boss is fine about it and I would like to present it to you next week when I am in Israel on other Church business.'

'Look, I am going to tell you what this other business is,' he continued. 'The Rev. Bill expressed a wish to be buried in a Christian cemetery in Israel. And it is down to me to finalise arrangements.'

Yossi was beginning to wonder if his suspicions had been unfounded. Maybe this Henry was on the level after all. In any case, if Ash had agreed he had no choice but to arrange a meeting and this was quickly finalised.

Just a few days later the front page of the Jerusalem Post contained a report of the Minister's funeral complete with a list of visiting and local dignitaries assembled to give him what they considered to be a suitable farewell.

Yossi was to meet Henry the following morning at the latter's hotel in Jerusalem. He was still trying to convince himself that the meeting had no threatening undertones for him when he arrived at the Ramada.

As soon as he entered the lobby, a tall handsome Black man who, quite unexpectedly, introduced himself as Henry Roberts, warmly greeted him. Yossi was surprised to be instantly recognised by the Church's security chief. He had no idea that Henry now possessed a close up photo of Yossi taken at the Church meeting when he had sat on the podium and expressed greetings to the entire assembly. Yossi had expected that he would have had to arrange for this Mr Roberts to be paged.

The pair entered the lounge and Henry suggested a corner table well away from the few other occupants of the room at that time of day.

Henry was self assured and confident and immediately produced a small parcel from his brief case that he handed to Yossi.

'Bill wanted you to have this as a small token of gratitude,' he began.

Yossi opened the parcel and Henry seemed to be as good as his word. It contained a small leather bound copy of the Old Testament and was inscribed: *With best wishes from Bill Cooper of the Church of the Second Coming.*

Yossi had no idea that Henry had discovered a further twenty-four identical bibles all prepared by the late Minister for people who had done some small service for the Church.

Yossi thanked Henry with as much enthusiasm as he could muster and prepared to take his leave.

'Hold it right there,' the Churchman said, 'you must join me in a quick drink if only to toast the memory of my boss.'

'Ok,' Yossi explained, 'but I must get back to work. Since the war in Lebanon ended, I am sure you will understand that we are inundated with new investigations.'

Both men preferred to drink black coffee and they sipped the hot dark liquid from the tiny cups as they savoured each mouthful.

'Now I really must go,' Yossi explained. 'Thank you again for the bible and for the coffee, but I am expected back at HQ this afternoon and it is a good two hours drive from here.'

Suddenly the previously smiling face of the black security officer clouded over.

'I am afraid there is something else that you and I have to discuss,' he said.

Yossi felt his stomach turn over. *Here we go,* he thought, *he knows all about the hold that the Rev. Bill had on me.*

'As you well know, the Church is a good loyal friend to the Jewish people. We are however, as aware as you are of the terrible dangers that fundamentalist Islam causes to both the Christian and the Jewish way of life.'

'Rev. Bill frequently warned us, as he warned all his friends, that we must be ready to do battle against these extremists. I now know that you are one of the few people on this planet who knows of the weapon that is available to us to destroy the enemy by pitting Sunni against Shi'a and Shi'a against Sunni in a way never seen before, even in Iraq.'

Yossi had been expecting some sort of blackmail attempt if this Henry had discovered the hold that the late Rev. Bill had over him. He had not, however, expected such a direct approach.

'What are you talking about?' Yossi replied. 'What weapon?'

Henry dropped his voice to a conspiratorial whisper and leaned towards the Mossad man.

'You know, the Baghdad Declaration,' he replied.

Yossi had reached the end of the line. If he knew about the scrolls then he would undoubtedly know about Yossi's two serious indiscretions while in the States. *This guy is tough and determined. If it suits him, he will shop me to Ash without a moments thought.* He agonised.

Yossi knew his only chance was to play for time.

'Ok, so you know about the scrolls,' he replied. 'I must tell you that Israel has no intention of using them. Any attempt to publicise them would end in disaster for all of us and particularly for Israel.'

'Well I don't agree,' Henry replied. 'These Islamists have to be stopped and this will sort them out once and for all.'

Yossi decided to try another tack.

'Look, we don't have the scrolls. Only one person, a British soldier knows where they are,' Yossi continued.

'Yes, I know that from Bill's notes, but you and I together are going to have to find them,' Henry replied.

'Look, I really must go,' Yossi answered.

'Ok, but I expect to hear from you with some kind of a plan. Shall we meet here tomorrow?' Henry conceded. 'I don't need to spell out the alternative do I?'

**The Safe House.**

James Smyth arrived the following morning. He explained to the two Manchester men that they were to be flown by helicopter to a small town just inside the area under American control. There, they were to be met by an SIS officer who would escort them in his armoured vehicle over the 'American' border and into the area controlled by Britain. It would then be the responsibility of Craig to direct them to the Cave of Ibrahim where the scrolls were hidden. Once the scrolls were located the two men had just one simple task to perform. The scrolls were to be destroyed.

Two other residents of the Safe House were desperate to discover the arrangements. It was obvious to both Prince Jamal and Professor Sa'id that the only possible reason for the presence in the house of Craig Blackburn, was to enable him to lead an expedition to recover the scrolls on behalf of the British government. Neither of these gentlemen was aware that a Mossad operative named Jack was in the house and would be accompanying Craig to the place where the scrolls were hidden. Furthermore they would have been horrified to discover the intention of the British and Israeli secret services, to destroy the scrolls. However, despite being fellow travellers in the quest to find the scrolls, the two Arabs had very different agendas to one another, once the scrolls were in their possession. The Professor wished to study them and have them placed on display in the Baghdad museum in which he worked. He had no desire to see them used in any political context.

The Prince however, was chasing a dream. He was now completely obsessed with a new golden age that he imagined for the Arab people and the world of Sunni Islam. Like his ancestor a thousand years earlier he was quite happy to let the Jews, or the Israelis as he now called them, have a piece of the Holy land. In any case he needed their military power to smash the Shi'a powerbases in Iran and the Lebanon. It was a blessing from Allah, he decided, that the new Prime Minister of Israel was his close personal friend Yigal Shomroni. However, he needed to completely discredit and destroy Shi'a Islam to achieve this agenda. If Iran, a non-Arab people, but the undisputed leader of the Shi'a world, was to discover the scrolls and the sympathy of his Sunni ancestor, An- Nasir, for the Jews, Iran would attack first and all would be lost.

First he must obtain the scrolls, then he must conclude treaties with the Israelis, the Egyptians, the Sunni populations in Iraq and Syria and yes, even the Saudis, although their kind of Sunni

Islam did not meet with his approval. He was sure his own people, the Jordanians, would rally to the cause and that his distant cousin the King would be delighted with him as a true son of the Hashemite family.

The two Arabs discussed how to find the scrolls, hour after hour and day after day. How could they discover the plans of their British hosts? They were certain that they must mount some kind of expedition to recover the scrolls. By a stroke of incredible fortune they were in the right place. Allah had smiled on them thus far. Would he continue to help them in their quest to commandeer the scrolls before the British, the Israelis or anyone else could get to them? The Professor worried, but the Prince had no doubt.

Then they had another stroke of luck. On the same day that James Smyth was giving his final instructions to Craig and Jack, the Prince, who had great difficulty in tolerating his self-imposed imprisonment, was in the lobby of the building. He hated being cooped up in one place and although the arrangements were comfortable enough they hardly compared with the incredible luxury of his villa outside Amman. He had taken to visiting the hallway of the building each morning to chat with one of the English security men. He had fond memories of his days in England and these conversations helped to keep him sane, or so he thought. Had any other person a modicum of knowledge of his mindset, they would certainly not have agreed about his total sanity. However, like most people with an obsession, he could converse quite normally on any subject other than the one that threatened his rationality.

James Smyth had arrived just a few minutes earlier with two escorts. One was a senior SIS man who accompanied him to his meeting with Craig and Jack. The other was a senior Iraqi policeman who had been recruited from the far more trustworthy ranks of retired Jordanian police officers.

When Prince Jamal arrived in the lobby he discovered this Inspector Ahmed already deep in conversation with a British Security Officer. The Jordanian immediately recognised the Prince. He briskly stood to attention and saluted.

'Your Royal Highness,' he began, with a look of absolute amazement. 'What are you doing here? Is there some kind of problem I can help you with?'

'No,' the Prince replied smiling. 'I came to Baghdad to visit an old friend and after an attempt was made on my life, I was offered sanctuary here by our good friends the British.'

'But Sir,' the Inspector replied, 'does the King and our government know of your visit. I am sure they would have dissuaded you from putting yourself in such danger.'

'Listen Inspector,' the Prince replied, 'I cannot tell you why I am here. It is a matter of top secrecy. I must forbid you from mentioning my presence here to anyone. My office and household in Amman believe I am away in Europe and that is the way it must remain.'

Like most Jordanian senior police and army personnel the Inspector always felt his first loyalty was to the Hashemite dynasty so when the Prince asked him why he was in the Safe House that day, Inspector Ahmed felt duty bound to tell his Royal Highness everything he knew.

'I am here to escort and protect a very senior SIS Officer who is visiting two members of his team in this building,' he told the Prince. 'I expect to be called in soon as I am to travel with the two SIS men tomorrow to the area under British control.'

'Will they have other officers from the Iraqi police in attendance?' the Prince enquired as nonchalantly as he could. He was very excited by what he had just heard. This was just the breakthrough he needed.

'Yes, your Highness,' the policeman replied.

'Can I rely on your complete loyalty?' the Prince demanded.

'Yes, of course,' the Jordanian replied.

'Do you realise that the interests of your own country Jordan come before any loyalty you may have for Iraq or America or even Britain?'

The Inspector nodded gravely.

'Of course your Highness, I am a Jordanian first.'

'Then this is what I want you to do...........'

### Jerusalem.

Yossi arrived the following day to keep his appointment with Henry. As soon as they were seated in a quiet corner of the hotel lounge, the latter began to issue instructions. There was no discussion. No enquiries as to how Yossi would cope with Ash if he learned of his indiscretions in America. There was just an apparent acceptance that Henry had Yossi in his power and therefore he was expected to obey him implicitly.

'Ok Yossi,' Henry began by dropping a bombshell. 'We are both going to Baghdad. I was there not so long ago and I have friends in the CIA who have agreed to arrange another trip for me. You will be travelling on an American passport. That will be ready later on today.'

Yossi gasped. His first thought was to wonder how this American could be so sure that Yossi would follow instructions. Then he realised ruefully that he knew exactly how Henry could be so sure.

The Mossad man had now recognised that this man brooked no argument or even discussion. He decided on a course of action and he saw it through. At least with the late Rev. Bill there had been conversation and although they both always knew that it was Bill who called the shots, the Minister would listen to Yossi's advice and consider the arguments put forward.

By the end of this meeting Yossi was certain that his career was in ruins. He decided that he could not and would not just disappear from the Mossad offices. He owed far more than that to his country, to the Mossad and to Ash. He resolved to listen intently to Henry and agree to follow all of his instructions. If he then went off to Iraq with Henry without some kind of explanation to Ash, his career would be finished anyway. And if his career was finished, he quickly decided, the time had come to make a full confession to Ash. He now had nothing and everything to lose whatever he did.

Yossi bade farewell to Henry and returned to the Mossad offices with a very heavy heart. All the way back he was turning over and over in his tormented mind how he was going to tell Ash of the situation in which he now found himself.

When Yossi arrived Ash was away from the station and did not return for another agonising three hours.

As soon as Ash entered his office Yossi knocked and opened the door. Ash was in a very good mood, having just been complimented by the head of the Mossad himself, on some recent work in identifying a cell of Hizb'ulla terrorists working abroad.

'Hi Yossi,' he said smiling. 'What can I do for you?'

'Ash,' Yossi began falteringly. 'We need to talk.'

Ash looked carefully into Yossi's face and could see that the younger man was in a nervous and deeply emotional state. This was not the confident Yossi he knew and he realised that what he was about to learn must be serious.

During the time anticipating this meeting Yossi had decided that he must tell Ash the full story from beginning to end.

As he recounted the events, starting with the Church meeting he had addressed and the story of how the Rev. Bill had compromised him with the woman called Jilly, the expression on Ash's face turned to one of anger and deep concern.

'I always knew that man was a phoney,' he exploded. 'The sanctimonious bastard really had you well compromised. However,' he continued gravely, 'you are a Security Agent employed by the State of Israel and you should have reported all this to me when you originally returned from the United States.'

'I have lots more to tell you,' Yossi sighed. He was beginning to feel some relief from the burden of keeping all this to himself for so long. He knew Ash was angry and he was certain his career in the Mossad was over, but at least he was now able to confess his sins.

During the first part of the story Ash's anger had largely been directed towards the Rev. Bill Cooper, of not such blessed memory. However, when Yossi told Ash of the meeting at the Bedouin café near Beersheba and how Cooper had forced him to give away information about the scrolls, Ash could contain himself no longer.

'Do you realise what you have done, you idiot? That information could lead to the deaths of thousands of people and seriously compromise the continuing existence of the State of Israel.'

'I know, I know!' Yossi replied, as near to tears as he had ever been as a grown man.

'I did persuade the Rev. Bill to keep this information to himself. I explained to him the gigantic dangers that would almost certainly occur if the content of the scrolls became publicly known. He did see our point of view and promised somewhat reluctantly not to pass the story to the media.'

'Oh well done,' Ash replied sarcastically. 'Talk about closing the stable door after the horse has bolted.'

'So,' Ash enquired wearily, 'is there more? There must be more. Bill Cooper is dead and you would not be here now if that was the end of the story.'

Before Yossi could reply, Ash interjected.

'Of course! Henry what's his name,' he all but shouted, 'I did think that was a bit of a funny story about wanting to give you a bible.'

'You are right, of course,' Yossi nodded sadly.

Now came the final act of repentance as Yossi told Ash of the events of the last few days.

When Yossi had finished Ash sat there motionless. Eventually he said quietly, 'do you think this Henry has told anyone else about the scrolls?'

'No,' Yossi replied. 'I am certain he has not done so. His idea is for he and I to go together to Iraq, somehow discover the whereabouts of the scrolls and obtain them before any of the other interested parties can get to them. Then I am certain he would publicise the texts.'

'I don't know if he loves the Jews the way Bill Cooper reckoned he did, but his hatred of Islam is fanatical. We are dealing here with a man as obsessed with his mission as Osama bin Laden is with his.'

Once again Ash became silent and thoughtful. This was not the reaction that Yossi had anticipated. He had expected to be instantly dismissed and probably arrested for giving away information prejudicial to the State.

The two men continued to sit in silence until Ash suddenly volunteered,

'Go to your desk and await further orders.'

Yossi rose to leave unable to comprehend why he had not been arrested and was not already on his way to jail to await trial for breaching state security.

**In the Iraqi Desert.**

The huge American helicopter touched down just three hundred metres outside the border of the large area of Southern Iraq that was the responsibility of the British forces. The massive rotor arm was still spinning as the giant machine started to discharge its human cargo. To two of the three figures watching the scene through binoculars, the sight of a dozen tiny figures jumping from the hatch and running bent almost double to a safe distance from the clouds of sand and dust was both familiar and compelling. It was familiar because both the Israeli Mossad man and the American CIA man had watched troops being landed, often in much larger numbers, from similar machines in Iraq, Israel, Lebanon and many other theatres of war. It was less familiar to the third member of the party, another American, a tall athletic looking Black man.

It was compelling to each of the threesome, but for different reasons. For Sam Browne of the CIA it was just a matter of repaying a favour to a good loyal American friend, a man he knew to be a patriot and a deeply religious senior member of Sam's church. However, although he could not and would not question his friend as to why he wished to be conveyed to this spot, it was compelling to watch the disembarkation from the distant helicopter, if only to try and ascertain why this particular troop lift should be so interesting to the black American and why they needed to spy on apparent allies from a distance.

To the Israeli it was compelling because the success or failure of his mission would chart the rest of his life, if there were to be a 'rest of his life' on this earth. There were just three possibilities for him on this trip. They were death, success or alternatively failure and disgrace.

To the black man, now dressed in the unfamiliar garb of a Gulf Arab, his compulsion was self-directed. The success of this mission formed an important part of his personal crusade against Islam and as he saw it, his entire raison-d'etre.

As the trio watched, two civilian members of the helicopter party were escorted to the largest and most heavily armoured Iraqi police vehicle. The third civilian from the helicopter, unknown to the observers, but actually a senior SIS man by the name of James Smyth, stood nearby, flanked by two Iraqi policemen. He watched warily as his companions parted company from him and set off upon their mission. The remaining members of the party comprised six men dressed as Gulf Arabs. They boarded two smaller police fortified jeeps, one leading and the other behind the larger vehicle. Within minutes the three Police vehicles were on their way in convoy.

The remaining civilian and his two-man uniformed Iraqi police escort then returned to the large American helicopter and were quickly airborne, flying North in the direction of Baghdad. As soon as they were certain that they had not been observed, the three men who had carefully watched the comings and goings of the occupants of the American helicopter proceeded to remove a camouflage net that had concealed their own small helicopter. This was hidden behind a convenient mound of sand. Within a further few

minutes they too were airborne and flying in the
general direction taken by the three Iraqi police
vehicles. It was not a particularly difficult task to
follow the convoy as there was only one fairly
narrow, poorly surfaced road leading South from
this point. It took but a further twenty minutes for
the observers to spot the convoy making clouds of
dust on the road below.

Sam Browne, the CIA man, was piloting the
aircraft and had the twin conflicting tasks of
keeping the convoy in sight and at the same time
to ensure that the people on the ground were
unaware of his presence in the skies behind them.
For two hours this strategy succeeded, but when
the police convoy suddenly came to an abrupt halt
and switched off their engines, Sam had to quickly
swing the helicopter round and fly speedily out of
earshot.

Craig had nearly missed the mound. Somehow
approaching it from the South made it appear
totally different. There had recently been violent
sandstorms in the area and the banking up of
sand and debris alongside the sloping walls of the
mound also tended to disguise it. They were
almost past it when Craig realised they had at last
arrived at their destination.

'Stop!' he yelled to their driver who quickly
jammed on his brakes nearly causing the police
vehicle behind to collide with them.

In the meantime the driver flashed his lights
frantically at the front escort vehicle and that too
skidded to a halt. The occupants of the rear
vehicle were Inspector Ahmed, seconded to the
Iraqi police by the Royal Jordanian Constabulary

and two apparently lower ranking native Iraqi police officers dressed for the desert as Gulf Arabs. One of these men thought for a second that he had heard the sound of a distant helicopter, but the bright blue desert sky appeared to be clear.

Meanwhile, back in the chopper, the black American, who was of course Henry Roberts, briskly took charge.

'Sam,' he instructed, 'as soon as we are completely out of sight I want you to land the helicopter.'

Sam was a loyal servant of the US government and only a request coming from an even higher authority, God, in the person of Henry Roberts of the Church of the Second Coming would have made him act other than in strict accordance with his instructions from the CIA.

Sam was on leave when Henry had contacted him and told him in no uncertain terms that the future of Christianity and Western civilisation depended on his co-operation with the Church of the Second Coming and its earthly representative Henry Roberts. Sam had never disobeyed an order from his superiors in the CIA and had been commended on many occasions for his loyalty and dedicated work for the Agency. However, with just a few minor misgivings, Sam had set about organising a US Passport for Henry's secret companion. Henry had also asked him to check on special transport arrangements requested by the British to ferry a person or persons from Baghdad to some point just inside the area policed by the UK. As a CIA officer he had access to all US information of this nature and quickly discovered that the very next day the British had requested their American allies to fly a party of men to some remote desert area. There were no other scheduled transport movements at any time that fitted the description that Henry had given him and a signal was sent to the Churchman. This had produced an immediate response with instructions to obtain a helicopter to convey Henry, his secret companion and Sam to the same destination.

Sam had now landed the small helicopter at a safe distance from where the convoy had stopped.

'Sam, you can stay here with the machine,' Henry ordered, 'We may need you to make a fast getaway,'

'My friend and I are going to see what is going on over there,' and he gestured in the general direction of the position of the convoy.

Sam was becoming more and more uncomfortable. He had carried out all of Henry's requests. He could not understand why they had not rendezvoused with the convoy rather than making themselves seem like an enemy to them. He could not believe that the Church would expect him to fight against America's friends. At this eleventh hour he began to wonder and to suspect the true motives of his friend, religious leader and mentor Henry Roberts. However, as he sat in the helicopter pondering where his real responsibilities lay, he decided to simply watch and wait.

Henry and his companion, who was of course Yossi, were now near enough to the convoy to recognise voices and decided to hide behind the large flat-topped mound nearby.

Once Yossi had reported to Ash the story of how he had been compromised by the late Rev. Bill Cooper, it came as a great surprise to him when Ash had told him to go along with everything that Henry ordered. As a result he had accompanied Henry to Iraq, met up with Sam and was now hiding with Henry to spy on a combined group comprising, as Ash had told him, a British sergeant called Craig Blackburn, his own Mossad colleague Jack and a detachment of senior Iraqi policemen.

Of all the men in either party only Craig had ever visited this spot before. It was therefore something of a surprise when he instructed just Jack to accompany him to the far side of the mound. He noticed that the two men dressed as Gulf Arabs in the rear escort vehicle seemed to be questioning this with Inspector Ahmed, but these two seemed intent on keeping well out of his earshot and the Inspector seemed to have told them to simply watch and wait.

Henry and Yossi had been concealed behind the mound and as soon as they realised that some of the convoy party were coming round to where they were hidden, they quickly made for some low scrub lying just fifty metres away. From this vantage point they hoped to be able to observe who was coming round the mound and for what purpose.

As they watched, two men, one of whom Yossi recognised as his Mossad colleague Jack, came in to view. They were carrying shovels and quickly started to remove sand that was banked up against the side of the mound. Very soon an archway leading into the interior of the mound was uncovered. A little more digging and the two men from the convoy were able to squeeze through and were lost in the interior darkness.

'Come on,' Henry said. 'That must be where the scrolls are buried.' Much to Yossi's horror Henry then produced a small machine pistol from under his jacket. However, before they could dash across to enter the cave two of the Iraqi policemen came round the corner and they too carried machine pistols.

Craig, now inside the cave with Jack, was shining his torch around, desperately trying to identify where he had buried the scrolls months earlier. It was then that they heard shuffling in the soft sand and realised that someone else was entering the cave. He nudged Jack and the two men hid behind a craggy outcrop in the wall of the cave. As they watched, the two Iraqi policemen who were dressed as Gulf Arabs from the rear car, crept inside the cave looking warily to left and right. Then one of them called out in perfect English,

'Are you two ok? We thought we had better come to help you.'

Craig and Jack kept silent. A shiver went down Craig's spine. I know that voice, he pondered. And then suddenly he realised the identity of the man who had just called out so solicitously. It was none other than His Royal Highness the Hashemite Prince Jamal of Jordan. Then Jack nudged him. He too recognised the beautifully enunciated English words. He mouthed 'Prince Jamal' and Craig nodded.

There was no doubt why the Prince was there. He obviously wanted the scrolls for his own purpose. But who was the other man? It was virtually impossible to communicate with each other, as the slightest noise would have given away their location. They certainly did not want to attack the new arrivals, particularly when one of them was a Prince from Jordan, a country having close links with Britain and a relatively cordial relationship with neighbouring Israel. However, before any decision could be made, a further pair of visitors came into the cave. They however, did not arrive quietly. The first one was a tall Gulf Arab or so his attire seemed to indicate, whom they had not seen before. Both Craig and Jack were certain that he had not been one of the men in the convoy. He was head and shoulders taller than any of them. He arrived brandishing a small machine pistol that he waved menacingly towards the Prince and his companion. The second man appeared to be unarmed and Jack realised with a shock that it was his Mossad comrade Yossi.

In the meantime the tall Gulf Arab flung back his headdress to show his face. He waved the machine pistol towards the Prince and his companion and shouted in a strong American accent, 'Back against the wall, you two!'

'Ok,' he then shouted, 'where are the other two. We know you are here. And we know who you are. Jack...Craig.... Come on out. Show yourselves. We are only here to help you.'

The two Manchester men remained silent in their hiding place.

'Come on out,' Henry again shouted. 'There is nothing to be afraid of.'

'Jack,' he continued. 'Don't you recognise me. I have already saved your life once in the shooting at the Al-Rashid Restaurant in Baghdad.'

Jack quickly reviewed the situation. They may have all arrived in this huge cave, but only Craig had any idea at all of where he had buried the scrolls in the soft sand. If Jack came out of their hiding place he could throw all the others off the track by saying Craig had gone deeper into the large cave to dig out the scrolls. He put his finger to his lips and signalled Craig to remain where he was.

'Ok.' Jack called. 'I am coming out now.'

All this time Yossi had kept silent, standing behind Henry and fingering the small automatic pistol in his pocket.

*'If this Henry makes any move to hurt Jack,'* he decided, *'he will get it in the back from me.'*

In the meantime the Prince had removed his headdress, but his companion still had his head and most of his face well covered. They were standing back against the wall of the cave where Henry could see them.

Jack walked slowly towards Henry and said,

'Yes, I do recognise you, but last time we met you had another name.'

'I certainly did,' Henry replied, 'and so did you.'

'You must know my companion,' Henry continued. 'I think you both work for the same firm.'

'We are all in this together,' Henry continued in a quiet voice. 'You Israeli guys must know that the

Church of the Second Coming is Israel's best friend.'

Henry then turned towards the two Arabs standing uncomfortably against the wall. 'Now what I want to know is who you two guys are.'

Neither Yossi nor Henry had ever seen the Prince unlike Jack who had visited his villa to unsuccessfully interrogate Craig. However, it was equally impossible to identify the Prince's companion and Henry suggested that this second Arab be requested to remove his headdress.

The Arab complied in the knowledge that none of these three men had ever seen him before. He knew that Craig would recognise him, but according to the Englishman the British sergeant was deep in the cave well away from where they were all standing near the entrance.

In any case this Arab was a gentle man, an academic and the idea of weapons being waved around by this black American disturbed him not a little. He had accompanied his friend the Prince as he wished to recover the scrolls for the benefit of Iraq and the academic research he could undertake with the scrolls in his possession.

The Prince considered Henry's request that they identify themselves.

'This gentleman,' he replied in his flawless English, 'is a Professor from Baghdad and I am here to assist him in the recovery of ancient documents being the property of the Government of Iraq.'

'And who are you?' Henry enquired, sensing that this man with his aristocratic bearing was more, much more than a just an assistant to the Professor.

The Prince considered this question and realised that if the Israeli Mossad man Jack was not disclosing the Prince's identity there was no reason why he should do so himself.

'I am an Iraqi businessman,' he lied. 'I have retired and I am working with the Professor as I wish to undertake studies for a degree in Iraqi history.'

This appeared to satisfy the black American and the Prince used the occasion to ask the three men standing before him to identify themselves. He, of course, knew quite well who Jack was, but the tall Black man who was calling all the shots intrigued him.

Henry, in reply to the Prince's enquiry introduced himself truthfully as Henry Roberts from the Church of the Second coming in the USA.

'And who are you two?' the Prince enquired.

Yossi replied, 'My name is Joe and I am here to assist Henry.'

The Prince was far from satisfied. 'You sound and look more like an Israeli to me than an American. I know who Jack is and he knows me. We have met before, haven't we Jack?' the Prince commented with a grim smile.

'Maybe,' Jack replied quickly, 'however, I think we are all here on the same quest so would it not be better if we all worked together?'

Craig had been listening to this exchange and felt confident enough to emerge now from his hiding place. He had arrived with Jack and of course he knew the Prince. He did not know the tall black man, Henry, nor the man who appeared to be an

Israeli and who had introduced himself as Joe. As for the second Arab, he had been unable to see him from where he had been hiding, but he was far from surprised to confirm his suspicion that the Prince's companion would be the Professor. When all was said and done he had seen him alive and well with the Prince in the safe house only ten days ago.

The Professor, feeling that the threat of violence had abated, if not totally disappeared, decided to take control.

'If we are all to work together to locate the scrolls, there are a number of conditions I wish to suggest.'

'First,' he continued, 'all weapons should be placed by the entrance out of harm's way.'

'Secondly,' he proposed, 'do we all agree that the ownership of these scrolls is vested in the Iraqi nation and that they should only be used for historical research?'

They all nodded enthusiastically although each of the men was secretly determined to stick to their own personal agenda.

Henry thought; *That might be your idea buddy boy. However, once we have found the scrolls Yossi and I will make sure that none of these others get their hands on them. I will then use them to set Sunni against Shi'a and Shi'a against Sunni until all of this evil doctrine called Islam is removed from the world. Then with all the Jews in the world gathered into Israel they will all be converted to Christianity to await the Second Coming of Jesus.*

Yossi thought; *I have promised Ash that the scrolls will be utterly destroyed so that they may not become another justification for violence.*

Prince Jamal thought; *I will use the scrolls to show the world that I am the true descendent and heir of the Caliph An-Nasir and that only the followers of pure Sunni Islam are the genuine inheritors of the way of life as preached by the Holy Prophet Mohammed. Shi'a Islam will be utterly destroyed together with the Wahabi distortion of the Sunni Muslim way of life.*

Jack thought; *Heaven preserve us from all fanatics. The scrolls must be destroyed before they send the entire Middle East and half the world up in flames.*

Craig thought; *these scrolls have put me through hell. Friends and foes alike have imprisoned me. My family and friends think I am dead and buried. All I want is to find these bloody scrolls and make sure they go up in smoke.*

**The Search**

There were only two shovels and that rather inhibited all six men joining in the search simultaneously. As Craig and Jack had brought the shovels, they started to dig in the area that Craig suggested. The other four members of the combined expedition wandered around that section of the cave pretending to inspect the tables and chairs unearthed by Craig on his previous visit. However, what they were really doing was keeping a very focussed watch on the two men who were digging. None of them trusted any other member of the expedition. As soon as the scrolls were unearthed every man present was prepared to fight to the death to ensure that he alone had the scrolls in his possession.

Craig remembered that he had buried them only a few centimetres under the sand. That was all that he had considered necessary at the time as the likelihood of anyone even finding and entering the cave, let alone starting to dig around in the soft dry sand, was remote. Then why could he not find them?

Eventually Henry and Yossi took over the task, but they too were unsuccessful. The Prince and the Professor after pacing up and down eventually decided that it was their turn. But the scrolls were nowhere to be found.

'Are you sure you buried them here?' Henry demanded of Craig.

'Of course I am sure,' Craig replied.

After a further period of frantic digging the Prince suggested,

'We are going about this in the wrong way. We are not being thorough enough. Let us start again at the wall and dig down say twenty centimetres in metre squares.'

'And where do we put all that sand?' Jack enquired.

'After checking each square metre we will have to put the sand back and mark the checked area,' the Prince suggested.

So the digging continued ever more frantically, but without finding any evidence of the presence of the two ancient documents they sought.

'Are you sure this is the right cave and the right place,' they kept demanding of Craig.

'Of course I am,' he replied time after time. 'I have worked just as hard as you people to find them and I really cannot understand where they can be.'

Inspector Ahmed had eventually decided to see what had become of the four members of his party. On entering the cave he was horrified to observe the spectacle of a Royal Jordanian Prince digging like a peasant in the soft sand, his shirt sleeves rolled up and his brow soaking with perspiration.

The Inspector was not aware that the other five men now knew the identity of the Prince and he strode over to speak to him in a low voice,

'You should not be doing this work, Your Highness,' he whispered.

The Prince, however, did not appreciate the policeman's solicitude and told him to return to the convoy immediately and not to enter the cave again.

Sam Browne sat in his helicopter listening to his radio, eating and drinking and trying to pass the many hours that had elapsed since his two companions had disappeared into the distance. He was familiar with spending considerable amounts of time in surveillance activities for the agency. However all that he was now doing was sitting and waiting and beginning to worry.

'I don't care how long we are,' Henry had instructed him. 'Your job is to stay put and have the chopper ready for a quick getaway.'

It was then that the news of the assassination of the Israeli Prime Minister came over the radio interrupting the programme with this serious news flash.

Sam had realised by his accent that Henry's companion was an Israeli. In addition with important news of this nature he knew that he himself would be required back at the CIA station in Baghdad.

*Whatever these two guys are up to,* he decided, *I have got to get them back to the chopper double quick. Or I will be for the high jump.*

Sam knew the general direction they had taken on foot and that they had probably gone to where the convoy had suddenly stopped. He started the engine of the aircraft and made to fly at very low altitude, just skimming the ground towards the flat-topped mound just visible on the horizon. A couple of minutes later he was almost relieved to see that the three-vehicle convoy was still in the same place. He dropped the machine on to the soft desert sand on the far side of the mound and away from the Iraqi police vehicles. Inspector Ahmed had just heard the news of assassination and was addressing his men when they heard the sound of Sam's helicopter approaching. However, with the mound in the way they could not see the aircraft and certainly they could not shoot at it. He marshalled his three men from the front escort vehicle and the four of them, automatic pistols at the ready, crept along the side of the mound. Sam was certain that the escort party would have heard him and he left the machine. He knew which way they would come to look for him and he started to call out repeatedly in Arabic, 'Salaam Aleikum.'

The Inspector and his men heard this call and Ahmed recognised that this was the voice of a British or American who had very little knowledge of the pronunciation of the Arabic language. He returned the greeting and signalled to two of his men to go round the mound from the other side while he and his Sergeant slowly approached the area where the unwelcome visitor appeared to be.

Sam then decided to take his life in his hands. He pocketed his pistol and raised his arms above his head and slowly turned the corner to confront the two Iraqi policemen.

Inspector Ahmed and Sam Brown had met before in Baghdad on at least three occasions when trying to deal with insurgents. They instantly recognised each other.

'I am looking for my companions,' Sam immediately explained.

'Describe them for me,' the Inspector answered.

'Ok,' Sam replied. 'One is a tall Black American wearing Gulf Arab robes and the other is a small dark-haired guy, also an American, but with an Israeli accent.'

'They are in the cave,' the Inspector explained.

'What cave?' Sam enquired.

'Inside here,' Ahmed answered, tapping the outer wall of the mound, ' but before I show you how to get in, have you heard the news?'

'You mean about Yigal Shomroni?' Sam answered.

'Yes and it looks like a pretty dangerous situation to me,' the policeman suggested.

'Well we had better go into the cave and tell them what has happened in Jerusalem,' the CIA man replied.

### Jerusalem.

Just the day before the six men had started their epic but fruitless search of the Cave of Ibrahim, a visitor had arrived to see the Israeli Prime Minister. She was an exceptionally beautiful example of Mediterranean or Middle Eastern womanhood. She was about thirty years old and of medium height. Her black hair was the perfect frame for her almond shaped face with its high cheekbones and sensuous dark brown eyes. She was decorously dressed in a long cotton skirt and a contrasting long-sleeved, high-necked blouse that made no attempt to hide the shapely contours of her delightful figure.

Prime Minister Shomroni rose to greet her when she entered his office.

'My dear Sheherazade or maybe you would prefer Leila?' he enquired with the tiny hint of a smile playing at the corners of his mouth.

'Leila is fine, Mr Prime Minister,' the girl replied.

'So let us get down to business!' the PM suggested as his eyes searched her face enquiringly.

'Where are they?'

Leila smiled in return and ventured,

'I assume you mean these, Mr Prime Minister?'

The young woman casually passed across the desk a most non-descript looking plastic supermarket bag.

Although the young lady was the personal representative of Asher Giladi of the Mossad she still had to have her handbag and all her possessions checked before being allowed into the office of the Prime Minister. A few eyebrows were raised by security as to why the contents of the plastic bag should be delivered to the PM but the items had been authorised by senior personnel.

As the Prime Minister examined the contents of the bag Leila sat quietly considering how she had won the scrolls for Israel. The clue had of course been the word 'Ibrahim.' It was not the name of one of the four terrorists who had imprisoned the British Sergeant Craig. Their names were Usama, Ali, Mahmoud and Fuad. Two of those violent men, Ali and Fuad, had been shot dead in front of Jack in the Al-Rashid Restaurant in Baghdad after successfully and sadly murdering the British agent Graham Jackson. That left her with Usama and Fuad, but still there was no Ibrahim in sight. After Jack had returned to Israel she pondered and pondered on what 'Ibrahim' could represent. The biblical Ibrahim or Abraham, as the Jews and Christians know him, was two thousand years before An-Nasir. She was sure that there would have been Abrahams or Ibrahims around at the time of the Baghdad Caliphate, but so what? That did not help at all.

Then she started to think about place names. In Israel there were a number of places linked with the biblical Patriarch, but in Iraq she could think of none. However, she decided to check an old atlas and there, North of Basra, she found a desert location clearly labelled 'Cave of Ibrahim.'

She was lost in these thoughts when the Prime Minister spoke again.

'Ok, Leila, are you going to leave these items with me until tomorrow? You know Ash has told me that our possession of these scrolls is top secret and I have assured him I will not disclose their presence here in Jerusalem to a living soul. I made a mistake discussing them with Prince Jamal and I will not make that mistake again.'

'Yes Prime Minister,' the girl answered. 'I was to impress upon you the danger of disclosure, but you have just said it all yourself.'

Shomroni rose and offered her his hand. He was far from being immune to the charms of beautiful women and would have much preferred a farewell kiss, but such are the penalties that high office imposes - only formal handshakes were appropriate.

Asher Giladi had known for a week that Leila had completed the hazardous trip to the Cave of Ibrahim disguised as a veiled Shi'ite Arab woman from the South of the country. He knew she had easily found the scrolls buried just inside the entrance to the cave, just as Craig had left them. They were under only ten centimetres of dry sand. It was immediately obvious to Leila that something had been buried there, as the level of the sand was higher than in the rest of that section of the cave.

Leila had signalled Ash via the Mossad listening post in Cyprus that she had found the scrolls and would return to Israel with them later that week.

In the meantime Ash had to decide what to do about the other plans he had set in motion. Jack Baker and the British sergeant Craig Blackburn were due to make their own expedition to the

Cave. He could not cancel their trip without alerting James Smyth of the SIS to the fact that the Israelis already had the scrolls. So their expedition had to proceed. Then there was the problem of Yossi, a first class operative who had allowed himself to be enmeshed in the plans of the late Rev. Bill Cooper and his even more unscrupulous deputy Henry Roberts. That trip also had to go ahead. In any case, Ash decided, both James and Yossi are going to have lots of extra information about their travelling companions when they return empty handed.

What the Mossad did not know was the intention of Prince Jamal to follow James and Craig to the cave. Nor was Ash aware that Professor Sa'id was alive and well and accompanying the Jordanian Prince on the journey.

### The Cave of Ibrahim

When Sam Browne and Inspector Ahmed entered the cave they were not accorded a rapturous welcome.

The Prince looked up and glared at Inspector Ahmed.

'I told you to wait with the other men no matter how long we are in here.'

Henry Roberts seemed equally irritated as he addressed Sam Browne.

'Sam, I did ask you to wait for us in the helicopter. What are you doing here?'

The six men had hardly had a good day. They were hot and sweaty, dishevelled and tired and all the digging had produced precisely nothing. They were still determined to find the scrolls, but the one who was most mystified by their inability to locate them was Craig. He thought he knew exactly where he had buried them, but where on earth were they now? For the last two hours he had begun to suspect that someone, somehow had been there before this expedition and unearthed them.

Sam Browne spoke first.

'Yigal Shomroni the Prime Minister of Israel has been assassinated,' he announced. Then with a glare at Henry he continued,

'I for one, must return at once to Baghdad.'

'And so must I,' Inspector Ahmed added.

The six cave excavators looked at each other. They knew they were beaten, but none of them were prepared to admit it. For some time now it had begun to look as if the scrolls were not in the cave, after all. And now with this news of the murder of Shomroni they had no choice, but to abort the mission.

All their private plans had come to nought.

Three of the men were not dissatisfied with the outcome. The two Israelis, Jack and Yossi felt that if they could not find the scrolls after such a thorough search, there was a good chance that no one else would either. It was an untidy outcome, but not an unwelcome one.

Craig was puzzled, but happy. He knew that he had buried the scrolls in the cave, but he began to doubt his own memory of the event so many months ago. Maybe he had buried them much further into the cave, but he kept those thoughts very much to himself. Anyway, there was no reason now not to allow him to contact his family in Manchester and nothing and no one was going to stop him now. They had mourned him for long enough and now deserved some good news. I would rather be jailed as a deserter he decided, than to be considered dead for a moment longer.

The Professor was deeply disappointed. He had lost the photographs of the documents on his computer months ago when his house had burned down. He would at least have had the pleasure of making an in depth study that way, in the absence of the originals. Now he had nothing. The Iraqi nation was going through hell and he had dreamed of giving them evidence of a golden age when Baghdad was ruled by the Caliphate.

The two other participants in the dig were heart broken. The Hashemite Prince Jamal saw all his dreams of becoming the new Caliph of a united Islam in ruins. It would however, have been a sad day for mankind if he had gained control of the scrolls and used them for his own purpose. Only a twisted mind could have imagined that starting a war between the Sunni and the Shi'a throughout the Muslim world would end in victory for the moderate Sunni. Anything could have happened and the carnage would have been too terrible to imagine, even in these bloodstained days.

The other fanatic was of course Henry Roberts. He saw a world where all its inhabitants had been forced or had agreed to become Christians. His mind was just as twisted as the Prince. Their agendas were different, one a fanatical fundamentalist Sunni Muslim and the other a fundamentalist Christian, but the ultimate effect would have been the same, war without end.

And so the unsuccessful expedition came to a sudden end and the men returned from whence they came. But that was not the last of the story of the Caliph's scrolls.

## Jerusalem

Security at Ben Gurion Airport, the Gateway to Israel was always tight. A nation that had been in a virtual state of war with many of its neighbours for the last sixty years and had been subject to countless acts of terrorism against its citizens, did not take chances. However, the two Israeli Arabs who arrived at immigration and passport control checked out perfectly. Their passports confirmed that they were brothers, Ismail and Yusuf Karim from Nazareth. They had been in England studying engineering at Leeds University. The young men were well dressed in fairly expensive casual clothing and thorough checking of the Immigration Control computer simply confirmed their identity. However, as subsequent events unfolded, it was discovered that they were not who they indicated themselves to be.

The real Ismail and Yusuf Karim were now at an Al Qaeda training camp in Afghanistan having been recently recruited while studying in England. Two other operatives who were already very experienced members of the organisation, having served the organisation in Iraq for two years, were now sent in to Israel on a top secret and vital mission.

Usama and Mahmoud were also Israeli Arabs, but preferred to think of themselves as Palestinians. They had both benefited from a comfortable middle class upbringing in a small village in Israel near to the Nazareth home of the real Ismail and Yusuf. They had joined Hamas, the Islamic party, while visiting family in Ramallah. It was then but a small step to Al Qaeda whose philosophy they embraced with great enthusiasm. When their training in Afghanistan had been completed they had been sent to Iraq to target the British and American occupation forces and the Shi'a Muslims who seemed intent on taking over the country. It was there in the company of Ali and Fuad that they had stumbled across Craig Blackburn sleeping at the side of a desert road. That had been a stroke of luck for them, but they preferred to see it as the hand of Allah guiding them. This of course, led them to the photographs of the texts of the scrolls that were stored on Craig's phone. When the matter was reported, the instructions from Al Qaeda were clear and unambiguous. We want all photographs, disks and paper copies containing images of the scrolls to be destroyed. And then we want the scrolls themselves delivered to the senior Al Qaeda representative in Iraq. Unfortunately Ali had already made a serious blunder in inviting Professor Sa'id to see the images on Craig's phone. The Professor immediately took over the interrogation of Craig and downloaded the photographs of the texts on to his own computer. The four Al Qaeda men had been forced to wait for an opportunity to destroy both the phone and the computer and this occurred after the Israelis had rescued Craig. To ensure that neither the Professor nor his assistant

Leila would suspect them, the house had been thoroughly gutted by a fire that the four men had started.

After that, the trail ran cold until a new recruit to Al Qaeda, an official in the British Embassy in Baghdad, reported that Graham Jackson, a senior SIS man, was due to meet a John Bradshaw for lunch that day. They had no idea of course, that this had any connection with the scrolls, but Graham Jackson had been far too clever in identifying and eliminating Al Qaeda members for some time now and was consequently someone they felt obliged to execute as soon as the opportunity presented itself. As luck would have it Ali and Fuad were in Baghdad having organised a suicide bombing the previous day. A watch was kept on the Embassy and when Graham Jackson and his companion set off for the Al-Rashid Restaurant, the SIS man's fate was sealed. However, that also resulted in the deaths of Ali and Fuad, but what is life in comparison with the paradise accorded to a Shahid? After the shooting another Al Qaeda man was despatched to the Restaurant and was able to extract from the waiter certain snatches of the conversation at that table where the words 'Caliph,' 'Scrolls' and 'Craig Blackburn' were mentioned. This made little sense to him, but once the report reached senior members of the organisation, details were sent back to Usama and Mahmoud. They, of course made perfect sense of the snatches of conversation.

Al Qaeda had not bargained with the disappearance of the Professor, but was aware from their informants in the ranks of the Iraqi police that his assistant Leila was now living and apparently studying in Baghdad. Periodic surveillance was organised and as a result, the unexpected trip to the South was discovered, but only when the young woman was on her return journey. Her behaviour when she arrived back at her apartment in Al Mansour and left again just a few hours later, clutching the same innocuous package with which she had arrived, was suspicious and when she left Baghdad Airport for Cyprus she was followed. At Nicosia the operative who had been following her was horrified to see her boarding a plane to Israel. He, in turn, sent a signal to a Palestinian whose cover was as a cleaner at Ben Gurion Airport, to look out for her. This was not a difficult task as even in a country of beautiful women, Leila, with her dramatically good looks, was instantly recognisable.

A further shock was in store for Al Qaeda. Leila was followed to a huge compound in the Negev desert known to be one of the main headquarters of the Israeli security organisation, popularly called the Mossad.

The next morning she was again followed as she returned to Jerusalem with the mysterious package, now partly obscured by being placed in a supermarket bag.

The final shock was when she delivered the package to the office of the Prime Minister.

In the meantime, Al Qaeda had despatched Usama and Mahmoud to Istanbul where they assumed their new and temporary identities as

Yusuf and Ismail Karim. They took the first plane out of Istanbul early that morning and took a taxi to Jerusalem to relieve their comrade waiting outside the Israeli Prime Minister's office. Just half an hour later Leila emerged significantly lacking the suspicious package.

Both Mahmoud and Usama were well ware of the contents of the scrolls and expected the Israelis to use the Caliph's Declaration as part of their title deeds to the land of Palestine. However they had no idea how they could gain entry, either by force or subterfuge, to a building of such importance.

That same afternoon, as arranged, Prime Minister Shomroni telephoned Ash at the Mossad station in the Negev. The conversation was of course on a totally secure line.

'Hi Ash,' he began. 'I have read and re-read the scrolls. I do think it would be a tragic mistake to destroy them. Historically and politically the day may well dawn when we would wish them to be made public. They are, however, absolutely unbelievable. If we are to keep their existence secret, how and where are we to store them?'

'Mr Prime Minister,' Ash replied. 'I have been considering the situation myself. I now believe that you are right that we owe it to the future never to deliberately destroy the past. However, if we have decided to keep them, the most secure location would be in Jerusalem. There are secret secure underground facilities just near the Shrine of the Book. That would be a safe and appropriate place to store the scrolls.'

'Ok,' Shomroni replied. 'That sounds good to me. Can you arrange collection?'

'Leila has remained in Jerusalem for this very purpose. I will have her round at your office within half an hour,' Ash quickly responded.

When Leila arrived, her return being carefully noted by Usama and Mahmoud, she was immediately ushered into Shomroni's office where he handed her the package, still in the supermarket bag. The PM then took the unprecedented step of personally escorting her to the entrance of the building. The waiting Usama could not believe his luck and completely ignoring the warnings of his companion he ran towards Shomroni firing repeatedly. The bag containing the scrolls was still in Leila's hand and there it stayed while she was ushered back into the building, now a seething mass of ambulance men, police, security men and military personnel. Usama was dead, shot at point blank range by Shomroni's bodyguard, but too late - the most popular, charismatic leader Israel had had for years was beyond the help of any agency on earth.

**Jerusalem-One Week Later**

The deputy Prime Minister now assumed the reins of power. He was a very different personality from his predecessor Shomroni. His name was Chaim Yosef and he was a member of a well-known Egyptian Jewish family who had left Cairo in 1956 to settle in the fledgling State of Israel. In Egypt they had been wealthy, but they had arrived in Israel virtually penniless. This was in the immediate aftermath of the Suez war when the Egyptian President Nasser and his government were determined to make the remaining Egyptian Jews pay for the sins, as they saw it, of their Israeli brothers. Their property was 'nationalised' and they were expelled from a country that had given them domicile for not hundreds, but thousands of years. With the exception of a small number of mainly poverty stricken elderly people, Egypt became a country without Jews. And of the large numbers forced to leave, most arrived in their new countries of domicile, Britain, France, the USA and Israel, as impoverished refugees.

Chaim's mother had arrived at the Israeli transit camp six months pregnant and Chaim was born later that year, still in the camp and the first Sabra (native born Israeli) of the family for probably two thousand years. Chaim was a quiet academic child who grew into a quiet academic youth and then into a quiet academic man. He was an unusual choice for a politician, but his brilliant intellect ensured that he was noticed at the Hebrew University by talent scouts who attended university debates on behalf of the Israel Labour Party. His quiet charm and sincerity endeared him to all and he rose quickly through the ranks of the party. As a party leader however, he was completely overshadowed by Shomroni who led the right of centre Likud. Now suddenly, this quiet gentle man found himself at the head of a coalition running a country that was resented and detested by many of its neighbours. His gentility however, hid a will of iron as he set about in his modest way to undertake the gigantic task before him.

After the assassination of Shomroni, a deeply traumatised Leila was ushered back into the building that housed the Prime Minister's office. There she was to await the arrival of her boss Ash. The Deputy Prime Minister, Chaim Yosef, had fortunately been in Jerusalem and arrived in the building well before the Mossad man who was flying up by helicopter. As soon as he entered, surrounded by a posse of Security men, he saw a still shaken Leila sitting in an outer office.

'I believe you were a witness to this terrible event,' he said.

Leila knew who Yosef was, but had never met him.

'Yes, sir,' she replied. 'It was terrible. I have been in many dangerous situations but the way this occurred was so totally unexpected.'

'I know you are very shocked, but I must ask you why you were here with the Prime Minister today?' Yosef enquired.

'Sir,' Leila replied, 'my boss Asher Giladi is on the way. He will explain it all to you.'

'Oh, do you work for the Mossad then?' the new Prime Minister replied.

'Yes Sir and I know Ash will be here within the hour and he will wish to report directly to you himself.'

Of course, the new Prime Minister had many weighty problems to deal with, not least the incredible security lapse that had allowed an Arab terrorist to get within firing range of Shomroni. When Ash arrived he was instructed to wait with Leila until a few minutes could be found to interview them. Even then, Chaim Yosef's primary initial interest was focussed on Leila's eyewitness account of the shooting.

Eventually the new PM said, 'Ok. Now let's discuss why you were here in the first place.'

Ash then told the story of the scrolls including the original decision to have them destroyed.

'That is amazing!' the new PM exclaimed in astonishment. 'And where are they now?'

'Here Sir,' Leila replied producing the plastic supermarket bag.

The Hebrew scroll was opened and Yosef read and re-read the beautifully calligraphed script.

'I agree we do not want to use this. We have more than enough turbulence in the area without adding to it.'

'However,' he continued, 'if we ever really have our backs to the wall it just could be something to consider, but only as an absolute last resort.'

'What I do not understand is what possessed Shomroni to tell Prince Jamal about the scrolls.'

'That is something we will never know now,' Ash replied sadly.

'Had you arranged somewhere for the scrolls to be stored away from the public eye?' the Prime Minister enquired. 'I want to be sure that there is no way that another living soul can become aware of the fact that we have these amazing links with the past, in our possession.'

'Yes Sir,' Ash replied. 'That was precisely why Leila was here today. She was to collect the scrolls and take them to a strong-room near to the Shrine of the Book.'

'Well Leila,' the Prime Minister responded. 'I know you were badly shaken by what has just occurred, but do you feel able to continue with your mission now?'

'Yes Sir,' Leila replied with a sad little smile.

'Leila, with all the crowds outside this building I am sure you can slip away quietly with your shopping,' Chaim Yosef continued, glancing at the supermarket bag now once again holding its priceless contents.

'You will be escorted for your own protection and that of your cargo.'

So Leila left the Prime Minister's office and within half an hour the Scrolls were safely locked away in the nearby building.

And Leila breathed probably the biggest sigh of relief of her not uneventful life.

**Basra.**

Craig had been returned to Basra after the debacle at the Cave of Ibrahim. From the point of view of British intelligence he ceased to be of any interest. Of all the people involved in the affair of the scrolls he was still the only one who had never been able to read and understand them. He had been warned never to discuss the matter with anyone. And that included his military superiors. Whatever had happened to the scrolls was certainly not something for which he could be held accountable. They had obviously existed as his photographs had proved. James Smyth had decided that if the scrolls could not be located after the exhaustive search, it was unlikely that anyone else would be able to find them. The SIS had devoted a considerable amount of time to the matter and now their efforts must return to the more pressing matters of Southern Iraq and Afghanistan, with its Al Qaeda links.

A suitable cover story had been invented by Smyth to explain the absence of Craig. This involved Craig being captured by dissidents and that was true. It also involved him being rescued by the SIS which was untrue, but the army in Basra was happy to have him back alive and well. There were not many stories in that part of the world that ended with a soldier being brought back from the dead. He was nevertheless severely reprimanded for disobeying orders in taking the road that ran alongside the mound. However, the Major who delivered the reprimand knew how deeply Craig regretted the incident and its resultant responsibility for the lives of his three companions. It was decided therefore that no further disciplinary action was needed.

Then Craig was allowed to make the most satisfying telephone call of his life. The one he had dreamed of making for so long.

'Mum,' he said when he heard the voice on the other end of the phone.

'Who is this?' a sad female voice enquired suspiciously.

'Don't you recognise your own son?' Craig enquired.

'Oh my God! It is you! It is Craig! They told us you were dead. We even attended your funeral although they said there was no identifiable body. Where are you?' she enquired without taking a breath.

Before he could reply she spoke again.

'Craig, it really is you, isn't it?'

'Yes Mum,' he answered happily. 'I was captured and rescued. I am coming home on leave next week.'

Sergeant Craig Blackburn had his leave and was determined to put away deep in the recesses of his memory, the past six months. He returned to duty in Southern Iraq early in 2007 and was killed by a roadside bomb just two weeks later. This time tragically he really was dead and his personal knowledge of the story of the scrolls containing the Baghdad Declaration died with him.

**Baghdad.**

Professor Sa'id was deeply disappointed not to have found the scrolls on the abortive expedition to the Cave of Ibrahim. His intentions had been strictly non-political. He was a mainstream Sunni Muslim and was certainly no fanatic. He was happy to consider members of the Shi'a sect as his brothers in Islam, providing they treated him with the same respect. His feelings for members of the Wahabi branch of Sunni were similar and in fact that toleration extended to Christians and to Jews. The Baghdad Declaration of the Caliph An-Nasir had fascinated him. This fascination was strictly academic and he had looked forward to examining the ancient forms of Arabic and Hebrew in the documents. The underlying political situation at the time of the Caliph An-Nasir also played a large part in his interest. He had even decided to have the parchment and ink on which the documents were drawn analysed. Now he was unable to undertake any of this research and he did not even have the photographs that might have satisfied his curiosity at least in terms of the styles of scripts and languages used. Craig's images had been completely destroyed in the fire that had razed his desert house to the ground. He was sure that if the Israelis or the British still had copies of the photographs of the two texts they would definitely not help him and would deny, for political reasons that they were in their possession. The only other place where the photographs might be stored was on the computer of Prince Jamal in Jordan. He had acted in a noticeably strange manner in recent times, but he still seemed to offer a better chance than Israel or the UK, to obtain photographs of the ancient texts. The Professor resolved to telephone Amman and ask his old college friend directly to prepare a CD that he would personally collect. That had the minor additional attraction of getting him away from Baghdad for a few days. The wholesale slaughter of the Sunni by the Shi'a and the Shi'a by the Sunni was breaking his heart. Why oh why, he conjectured did his beloved Iraqi people have to behave like this?

The telephone rang in the Prince's villa. The same impertinent servant as last time answered it. Again the Professor said he was a friend of An-Nasir, but this time the servant refused to put the Prince on the line. According to this man the Prince was ill and was not to be disturbed. Furthermore he indicated that he could give no date in the immediate future as to when Prince Jamal would be well enough to speak to the Professor. Professor Sa'id replaced the handset with a heavy heart. He assumed that the Prince had developed a serious physical illness, maybe some kind of cancer, since he had last seen him in the Cave of Ibrahim. He resolved to telephone another old Jordanian friend who was a member of the government. Once he mentioned Prince Jamal the voice on the other end of the line suddenly became very guarded and unfriendly. This contrasted with his original greeting to the Professor when he realised it was he who was on the line. At that stage he had responded with warmth and pleasure.

'Look Abdullah,' his friend told him. 'You had better forget any idea you had of getting in touch with Prince Jamal. He is sick, very sick and is not allowed any visitors or phone calls. That is all I can tell you.'

The following day, as the Professor left the museum where he worked, he suddenly became aware of someone walking close behind him, far too close. He turned to discover with a shock that Mahmoud, one of the four men who had captured Craig Blackburn and started this whole sad affair, was his unwelcome companion.

'Salaam Aleikum, Professor,' Mahmoud greeted him. 'We need to talk.'

The Professor had no wish for this man's company or conversation. When Craig had been a prisoner it had suited Abdullah to use Mahmoud and his three companions as guards. In any case he had no means of ridding himself of them without arising their suspicions that he was not really in sympathy with their cause or behaviour.

Now, at this time, this Mahmoud was one of the last people on earth he would have wished to meet, whether outside the museum or anywhere else.

'Salaam Aleikum,' the Professor replied and made to walk away from the man who had just accosted him.

'Professor, we need to talk,' Mahmoud repeated.

The Professor glanced down to see that Mahmoud was clutching a handgun.

Abdullah's voice was quaking as he reluctantly suggested. 'Come back to my office in the museum.' He was not a brave man when faced with a known terrorist carrying a gun. A life in academia, even under the vicious regime of Sadam Hussein, does not equip you to do deal with such eventualities.

Once in the Professor's small office Abdullah decided that he must appear warm, friendly and cooperative. This decision was more than partially influenced by the fact that the handgun was now on the Professor's large desk and within easy reach of the man sitting opposite him.

'Now, Mahmoud,' he began. 'What can I do for you?'

Mahmoud wasted no time in getting down to business.

'I am instructed to delete or destroy all copies of the photos of the filthy evil blasphemous documents that were on the British soldier's phone.'

The Professor felt oddly relieved. Surely this man would know that both his computer and the soldier's phone had been destroyed in the fire at his home. He quickly pointed this out to Mahmoud who nodded in agreement.

'So what do you want with me?' Abdullah enquired.

'You know who else has copies of the photographs of the texts on file and we need to find them,' he replied.

The Professor considered the demand and decided that there could be no harm in giving this man at least some information. He would give him just enough to send him on his way, as far away as possible.

'I don't think the British have them and I am sure the Americans don't. They have not been involved in this at all. Maybe the Israelis have them, but if they do I cannot help you there.'

'Come on, who else?' Mahmoud replied. 'We will deal with the Israelis in our own way. Who else?'

'No one I can think of,' the Professor lied.

'I think you are now lying to me,' Mahmoud commented. 'Come on, who else?'

'Our organisation knows you were in a British safe house, as they call it, here in Baghdad. We also know that you went there with Prince Jamal of Jordan. He must have the pictures of the texts.'

Professor Abdullah Sa'id was not a good liar. He was an excellent archaeologist and researcher and given the place and time, a sincere human being. At the mention of Prince Jamal he looked exceedingly uncomfortable, but again denied the suggestion.

By this time the two men were alone in the huge building and Mahmoud was fast losing patience.

He raised the handgun and pointed it directly at the Professor's head and repeated,

'Who else? If you do not reply and tell me the truth I am going to blow your head off.'

The Professor had still not discovered any inner reserves of courage and he broke down in tears.

'Yes, yes, Prince Jamal is the only one I know of anywhere in the Arab world who has the texts on his computer.'

'Thank you Professor,' Mahmoud replied as he stood up to leave, 'and this is for you.'

His gun had been pointing at Abdullah Sa'id throughout this exchange and now he emptied the chamber in to the Professor's head and body leaving a bloodied corpse to be found the following morning.

**Amman. Jordan.**

The behaviour of Prince Jamal had been giving cause for concern for some time. As a result he was under increasing scrutiny. There had been evidence of irrational conduct on a number of occasions. He had previously been a reliable spokesman on behalf of his country, particularly in matters relating to Jordan's relationship with Israel and the UK. In the period immediately before he had been made aware of the existence of the scrolls, however, he had suddenly made a number of wild and inaccurate statements to members of the Jordanian government. These included severe and totally unjustified criticism of the King and even of his late and beloved father, King Hussein. As a result his public speaking engagements had been cancelled and he no longer received sensitive government information and reports. In addition it had been considered wise to replace one of his servants with Hassan, who was a member of Jordanian Intelligence. He reported back to a senior officer on any and all evidence of strange conduct. He had, of course answered the telephone when the late Prime Minister of Israel had phoned the Prince and although unaware of the details of the conversation, he had reported this contact. Then there was the matter of the strange meeting that had taken place in the Prince's office with a young British man, who looked like a soldier, and two Israelis. Finally there was the visit of the Iraqi man who described himself as the friend of 'An-Nasir.' As a result of these reports, permission was given to install listening devices. However, before these were in place the Prince had disappeared. The authorities decided that as long as the Prince was not making public statements they had no cause for concern. That was until they were horrified to discover that he had been reported as having been sighted in a hotel in Baghdad. It was impossible to ascertain what he had been doing there and then once again he disappeared from view. This time it was for some weeks, but as long as he was out of the public view the Government and the Royal family were relieved.

Now he had returned and although no longer meddling in affairs of state, he seemed to have assumed a gravitas that indicated that he considered himself to be of a rank far higher than that which he enjoyed in reality. He was a third cousin of the King once removed and he had instructed his entire staff to bow low before him and to ask his permission before even speaking to him on the most mundane of subjects. He gave the impression that he considered himself to be an all powerful ancient Emperor or Caliph.

Three prominent Psychiatrists were sent to see him and reported back that he had become dangerously deranged.

The Prince was placed under house arrest, but he hardly seemed to notice as his dream world filled more and more of his existence.

Had the Prince mentioned the scrolls of the Baghdad Declaration he would never have been believed anyway. However, the photographs were still on the hard drive of his personal computer.

Because of his isolation and strange behaviour, visitors had become a rarity. Hassan was more than a little concerned when he answered the telephone to someone who spoke little or no Arabic and had a strong English accent. When challenged he explained that he was an old friend of the Prince and could he please speak to him.

'What name shall I say?' Hassan enquired.

'Tell him John Bradshaw. We were at university together in England,' was the reply.

'The Prince is far from well, I am afraid and is not receiving phone calls or visitors,' was the reply.

By this time news of the mental state of Prince Jamal had filtered through to the Mossad. Ash had hardly been surprised. The Prince's insistence on keeping to himself the news of the scrolls may have been very much to the liking of the Israelis, but it was hardly a rational way to approach matters from a Jordanian standpoint.

So Jack in the disguise of John Bradshaw had been instructed to make contact. The Mossad needed to be sure that the Prince was sufficiently deranged not to be taken seriously if he started to discuss the scrolls and somehow they needed to wipe the photographs of the texts from the Prince's computer.

They had no need to worry however, as help in deleting the photographs was at hand from an entirely different and unexpected source.

A new cleaner had just been employed in the Prince's household. It was somewhat strange that an Israeli Arab would want such a job, but he seemed to be reliable and the task of the Jordanian Intelligence was keeping the Prince quiet, not particularly protecting him from unknown and unspecified dangers. This was role reversal. A year or two earlier, when the Prince was well enough to represent his country, great care had been taken to keep him safe. Now it was more to protect everyone else from the Prince's irrational behaviour that was the priority.

Mahmoud, or Yusuf Karim, as his passport stated, was now the only remaining member of the four-man team of Al Qaeda operatives who had snatched Craig and discovered the photographs of the texts on the mobile phone. After the murder of the Israeli Prime Minister by his brother in arms, he had nonchalantly wandered away from the scene in company with the large crowd now dispersing after the tragic event. He had his Israeli ID card and easily passed road blocks and check points hastily assembled by the police after the assassination.

First Al Qaeda had instructed him to visit Baghdad with tragic results for the late Professor Abdullah Sa'id.

Now he had been instructed to go to Jordan, a Sunni country, but considered to be too friendly by far with Al Qaeda's enemies, Israel, the USA and the UK.

As a cleaner he had access to most of the rooms in the villa. It was only if the Prince himself was in a particular room that Mahmoud was forbidden to enter. His main task was to locate the study where he assumed he would find the computer. Three days after starting his job, in the knowledge that the Prince was reading in one of the lounges, he entered, complete with cleaning trolley and immediately located the state-of-the-art HP processor on a desk at the end of the large room. The machine was switched off and Mahmoud pressed the button on the computer to bring it to life. At the same time he switched off the monitor, just in case someone should enter and wonder why the computer was active. He then set about his cleaning tasks and after five minutes or so, he approached the processor again and reactivated the VDU. There was nothing unusual to be seen. The 'My Pictures' icon was there on the desktop and he clicked on it. Again he switched off the monitor to satisfy himself that no one was approaching in the corridor outside. Returning again he quickly found a folder labelled 'An-Nasir.' That had to be the one and yes, there were the Arabic and Hebrew versions of the Declaration. Deleting them was easy and he was just about to shut down when someone entered the room. He spun round to see Price Jamal himself standing there.

Quickly he pulled out the same handgun that a week earlier had murdered the Prince's friend Abdullah Sa'id. It took only seconds to despatch the tormented soul of Jamal to Paradise and only a few more seconds for Mahmoud to follow him by courtesy of Hassan, the man acting as the Prince's servant.

The Prince was buried that same day in accordance with Muslim tradition and accorded the great respect reserved for members of the Hashemite dynasty, even third cousins of the King.

All electronic evidence that the Baghdad Declaration had ever existed was now destroyed in the Kingdom of Jordan.

**Dallas.**

The elders of the Church of the Second Coming had decided that the Gospel according to their late leader the Rev. Bill Cooper must continue to be preached. Most of them felt, however, that Bill was irreplaceable and it was decided that a group of three or four of their best preachers would again organise rallies around the USA, just like in the old days. All of them would give sermons to the faithful in the absence of any one single speaker considered to be gifted and charismatic enough to spread the word alone.

The Elders had also decided that Henry Jackson would take full time responsibility for all administrative, political and security matters with the title of Governing Administrator. He would not speak at rallies, but in almost every other respect he was to act as the leader of the Church. He was also in overall charge of publicity and representatives of the media wishing to interview any preacher privately were to have their requests cleared by Henry.

Henry had returned to the USA deeply disappointed that the scrolls had not been found. He had, of course, no idea that they were now safely residing in Jerusalem. His hatred of Islam was as strong as ever, but his first responsibility was to the Church of the Second Coming.

The Preachers were in Dallas and the rally was due to take place in the giant NFL Texas Stadium. Henry had made a point, since his new appointment, of always accompanying the preachers to ensure that all the arrangements made by his staff were in order. Everything was fine and although the huge stadium was not full, there were tens of thousands of people there who had travelled from far and wide to the event. As always there were a few reporters from national and local newspapers. A few months earlier, when the attraction had been the Rev. Bill Cooper, the crowd of representatives of the Press Corps would have been much larger. It was a rare rally when the late Minister did not give them a juicy and often sensational quote or two for their readers.

The three preachers present were modest and moderate men as befitted their calling. They preached the 'word' as they saw it, in a manner that was very different to their late leader. In fact the last speaker in Dallas on this particular day had often been troubled by the aggressive tone adopted by the Rev. Bill, especially when discussing Islam and Roman Catholicism. His name was the Rev. Ivor Jones and he was the son of Welsh Methodist immigrants.

It was customary to take questions from carefully selected members of the media at the end of each rally and the last question on this occasion was allocated to Wayne Aziz of the New Jersey Observer. Wayne's name had always been a subject of debate and some amusement when he was out of earshot. Aziz certainly sounded like a Muslim name, but Wayne was the category of first name that was popular with Americans born fifty and more years earlier. It was certainly not the sort of name given to a nice Muslim boy.

'Would the Rev. Jones be prepared to comment on the continuing bloodshed in Iraq involving both the Sunni and Shi'a communities and our brave American soldiers caught up in the crossfire?'

'Thank you for that question,' Rev. Jones replied. 'The sectarian violence in Iraq is a tragedy of monumental proportions. We must all pray that with the help of the Almighty, peace will again prevail.'

The Preacher paused as he examined the faces of the assembled Church members, nearest to him. Then he decided to take the plunge in a manner that would have horrified his late leader.

'We must remember, he continued, 'we are all children of our Father in Heaven, Jews, Christians and Muslims as well. We all worship the same God, there is only one true God and he is the God of us all. Our paths to salvation may be different, but we are all brothers.'

Henry heard this pronouncement from the audience. He always liked to stand among the people so that he could report back on the crowd's reactions to the speeches and sermons. He was deeply shocked by what the Rev. Jones had just said. There was no way that Henry could accept any kind of brotherhood with Islam. The session of questions was supposed to be over, but, throwing caution to the wind in his anger, Henry grabbed a microphone from one of the stewards and shouted out in the earshot of the entire assembly,

'How can you say that? The people killing each other and killing good Christian American Servicemen are no brothers to us.'

The Rev. Jones instantly recognised Henry's voice. However, he may have been a quiet gentle man, but he loved God and all humanity in the spirit of his own religion and he had been longing to spread his own message of brotherly love that so much contradicted the words of his late leader.

'When Muslims do evil things I condemn them utterly. However, I also condemn all who do evil, whether they are Christians, Jews or Muslims. That is not the way of the Lord.'

Henry was fast losing control. Saying anything positive about Islam was for him, like touching a raw nerve.

'Don't you realise,' he bellowed, 'that it is their religion that makes them into fanatics and evil doers?'

The huge crowd was astonished. Many of them had been brain washed for years by the Rev. Bill's pronouncements. They could not believe that one of his preachers should have spoken thus. As for the Press Corps, they were delighted. The meetings of the Church of the Second Coming had become far too tame in recent months. Now some real controversy was developing.

Henry was in full flight.

'I curse the followers of Islam and so should you. They have brought nothing but bloodshed and evil to the world. What about 9/11? What about Madrid? What about London?'

And then came the thunderbolt.

'Good people, do you know that the Sunni and Shi'a have been fighting each other for over a thousand years? Do you know that an evil Sunni Caliph tried to trick our Jewish friends into supporting him at that time against the Christians and the Shi'a? Thank God the Jews did not fall for it. Gentlemen of the press, I know all about this, just come and ask me,' he finished.

The Rev. Jones sat down wearily. *What on earth is Henry talking about and what a meal the newspapers will make out of this*, he conjectured.

The Rev. Johnny Winchester, the Chairman of the meeting stood up.

'That is the end of the proceedings for today. May the blessings of God Almighty be with you. Go carefully and go in peace.'

The crowd started to disperse except for a handful of members of the media who smelled a story in the wild pronouncements that they had just heard from Henry.

Once the huge stadium was empty the small group of reporters followed Henry into one of the offices.

Henry decided to lose no time in explaining. The knowledge of the existence of the Baghdad Declaration had been gnawing away at him ever since he had discovered all the details.

'A document has been found,' he began, once the pressmen were settled. This was as far as he got when there was knock at the door.

'Come in,' he called assuming it was yet another reporter and a tall black man, not unlike himself in appearance, entered the room. He was smiling broadly as he said,

'Hello Henry, what kind of a lousy brother did you turn out to be?' He was still standing with his back to the open door as Henry gasped, 'Eugene, I thought you were dead.'

'No, I am very much alive, thank God, but you the sworn enemy of God and his Holy Prophet are about to die.'

The two members of the Press Corps nearest to him leaped towards him, but too late, he had emptied the magazine of his machine pistol into his brother, who died instantly.

The Al Qaeda man struggled like a cornered animal to free himself from the reporters who held him, but in vain and within minutes the police had arrived. Henry had breathed his last and had died at the hand of the brother who was largely responsible for his hatred of Islam. It was then discovered that Eugene, or Ismail as he now called himself, had been strapped up with a bomb that miraculously had failed to explode.

Otherwise the press corps would have been sadly and tragically depleted by this act of fanatical lunacy.

In the course of questioning he was proud to admit to the murder of the Rev. Bill Cooper and is now awaiting sentence in the USA for a number of terrorist crimes.

**The Survivors.**

And so the scrolls that contained the Baghdad Declaration, remained securely locked away in their secret location near the 'Shrine of the Book' building in Jerusalem. Ash and Leila of the Mossad and the new Prime Minister of Israel, Chaim Yosef were the only people to know of this fact. Neither Jack Baker nor Yossi was ever privileged to learn of their location. The electronic vault coordinates to gain access were changed daily and were signalled in code every morning to the Prime Minister's computer. This system worked perfectly until the hard disk of the processor that created these coordinates mysteriously and unaccountably crashed in March 2007. After that, no amount of effort to discover how to open the vault electronically yielded a result. Even the original supplier of the software was unable to find an answer. After numerous meetings with Ash on this subject it was decided that the only way to gain access to the tiny vault would have been by using the latest cutting equipment. The amount of heat generated would have seriously damaged if not destroyed the scrolls within the vault. Eventually the problem was put on hold. Two sets of documents telling the entire story of the scrolls were then prepared by Ash and are now stored in a secret secure location elsewhere, together with disks containing Craig's photographs of the texts.

When Yossi's indiscretions were re-considered by Ash and other senior Mossad officers he was asked to discreetly resign. Only one month later, while employed as a security guard outside a Tel Aviv bank, he was gunned down.

Jack, on the other hand, was promoted in the Mossad. He had always admired Leila for her beauty, intelligence and sincerity. Indeed he had to admit to himself that he had been in love with her ever since their paths had crossed. However, working together in the same organisation precluded a relationship and he was forced to worship her from afar. When she decided to retire from the organisation they started to date and by the spring of 2007 she had become Mrs. Jack Baker.

The Declaration of the Caliph may or may not have been made in good faith, but the tragic loss of life that occurred at the time when the scrolls were prepared was repeated in the present day. Whether the Caliph would have honoured his declaration to install a Jewish Kingdom in the Holy Land or whether this was just a ruse to obtain the support of world Jewry was never put to the test. Judging by the fate of most of the participants in the affair, the scrolls were cursed and the day when Sergeant Craig Blackburn had found them turned out to be a tragically sad day not only for him, but also for many other people.

However, had the contents of the scrolls been divulged, the result would have been unimaginably worse. We should all pray that they will stay in their present inaccessible hiding place until the arrival, if ever, of a better and more peaceful world.

**END.**